JOURNEY

The compelling tale of a
journey to America 1720

Shirley A Kitner Mainello

authorHOUSE®

AuthorHouse™
1663 Liberty Drive
Bloomington, IN 47403
www.authorhouse.com
Phone: 1-800-839-8640

Published by AuthorHouse 03/28/2013

ISBN: 978-1-4817-2757-0 (sc)
ISBN: 978-1-4817-2758-7 (e)

Library of Congress Control Number: 2013904780

Any people depicted in stock imagery provided by Thinkstock are
models,
and such images are being used for illustrative purposes only.
Certain stock imagery © Thinkstock.

This book is printed on acid-free paper.

Because of the dynamic nature of the Internet, any web addresses or
links contained in this book may have changed since publication and
may no longer be valid. The views expressed in this work are solely those
of the author and do not necessarily reflect the views of the publisher,
and the publisher hereby disclaims any responsibility for them.

Dedicated to

all those brave

immigrants who

came to our shores

and devoted themselves

to building the county

we enjoy today.

Thank you.

Journey

Table of Contents

Journey vii

Forward xiii

Germany 1

    One 3

    Two 10

    Three 17

    Four 23

    Five 30

    Six 40

    Seven 45

    Eight 51

    Nine 56

    Ten 59

    Eleven 63

    Twelve 67

Down The Rhine 71

    Thirteen 73

Fourteen 78

Fifteen 84

Sixteen 87

Seventeen 92

Eighteen 96

Nineteen 99

Twenty 105

Twenty-One 110

Rotterdam 117

Twenty-Two 119

Twenty-Three 127

Twenty-Four 133

Twenty-Five 137

England 143

Twenty-Six 145

Twenty-Seven 152

Twenty-Eight 156

Twenty-Nine 160

Thirty 163

Thirty-One 165

The Atlantic 169

Thirty-Two 171

Thirty-Three 175

Thirty-Four 179

Thirty-Five 183

Thirty-Six 187

Thirty-Seven 192

Thirty-Eight 194

Thirty-Nine 197

Forty 200

Forty-One 205

Philadelphia 209

Forty-Two 211

Forty-Three 215

Forty-Four 218

Forty-Five 222

Forty-Six 226

Forty-Seven 228

Forty-Eight 230

Forty-Nine 234

Epilogue 1771 237

Historical Background 241

To Read More On This Subject 247

About the Author 251

Books By This Author 253

Book Club Guidelines 255

Forward

This tale of three fictional immigrant families, who lived near the Rhine River in the early 1700's, is based collectively on the experiences of the thousands of immigrants who came to America from that area, called the Palatinate, between 1700 and 1760.

The Meier family consists of two older brothers, Wilhelm and Peter, Katja, a sister of nearly seventeen years, two smaller brothers, Daniel and Jorg, and a little sister, Inge about three years. The paternal grandfather is also a part of this family. The parents have died of war and disease, however, the family survived together with hard work and love for each other. The older brothers became the head of the family. Katja took the responsibilities of a mother to the younger children.

The Holtzmann family includes Ulrich with his wife, Barbara, and their young son, Johannes who is a toddler. Ulrich is a talented carpenter who is literate enough to do his kind of work. Barbara comes from the same kind of illiterate farming background as the Meier family.

The Kramer brothers, Jakob and Hans, live with their mother who is very ill. The young men own and operate a village store which has been in their family for generations selling produce from the farms and shops of the area. They are literate and have been educated about the world by their father, who had spent some time as a sailor.

Life, as they experience it in that difficult time in the Palatinate, forces these families to plan a journey to Amerika. That journey takes them from their homes, down the Rhine to Rotterdam, then on to England. They continue across the Atlantic in the ship, the *Good Queen*, and finally up the Delaware River to Philadelphia, a city of about twenty thousand in 1720.

Readers get involved in the struggle such a trip entailed and the sacrifices these immigrants are forced to make in order to fulfill their dream.

If your ancestors came from Germany, Switzerland, Alsace, or northern France in the 1700's they may have experienced any or all of the things the families in this story endured.

It is a tale to touch the heart of a historian, genealogist, or a fan of well researched historical fiction.

Germany

Near Mosbach

One

THE MOMENT THE PRINCE Elector's wagons rolled up to the grain storage shed, the loud-mouthed overlord began directing the division of grain, hay, beans, apples, and other produce from Fall harvest on the Meier farm. Standing on his wagon seat, pointing with his fat finger to the freshly made hay stacks, he shouted, "Load two of the three stacks!"

The Prince's workers hurried to do his bidding, lest they become the recipients of his wrath. They knew it was best to just keep your head down and do what the overseer asks.

Wilhelm and Peter Meier had been though this every year of their lives. When the Prince sent his men to collect his share, it became a time of anxiety and tension. The two brothers helped with loading, to make sure they could save enough to last their family through the winter. They knew they had to swallow their pride and pretend to cooperate.

Shirley A Kitner Mainello

They had extra hay hidden above the goat's stall and more grain hidden in large crocks buried under the ground.

The two brothers were strong well-built young men who farmed for the owner of the land, the Prince Elector, who took a large share of all they produced. Such farmers worked under the close supervision of Overlord Frederich or people like him. It was better to let the overlord feel his power; the sooner he was gone, the better.

As soon as the hay was loaded, the soldiers yelled, "Bring that other empty wagon up to divide the grain!" The four soldiers, who came along to control any farmer who became uncooperative, eyed the bins of grain, mentally dividing it into three parts, two of which were to be taken by the Prince Elector. The workers, dressed in homespun shirts and worn lederhosen, started shoveling the grain from the bins. They did their work without comment.

Again, Wilhelm and Peter appeared to cooperate by helping, they didn't want to give the overlord any reason to search the farm which would happen if he thought they were holding back some produce.

Next, Overlord Frederich inspected the animals. "I see you have five pigs; we will take the three large ones!"

One of the soldiers walked over to Wilhelm and growled, "Where are you hiding the sheep?"

"The sheep are in the pasture on the hillside as always," Wilhelm replied keeping his voice calm and even.

"We will be back in Spring when you shear them. Don't forget the Prince gets his share of the wool!" he snarled, as he stroked his ugly, dirty beard, wiped his hand on his uniform. He turned his horse and rode to the front of the wagons.

Wilhelm and Peter breathed a sigh of relief as the group began to drive away to collect their share from the next farmer. They exchanged silent glances with each other. Overlord Frederich, would not have liked the secret plans the brothers were making this very evening in this same small barn.

❀　　❀　　❀

After supper, the friends gathered in the cow shed quietly making their special plans. The soft light of the lantern shown on their faces as Wilhelm and Peter Meier told Jakob and Hans Kramer, brothers who had a store in the village, about Overlord Frederich's visit. The lantern light lent an ominous, secretive feeling to the discussion casting its glow on the young men whose lives had been filled with hard work since childhood.

Ulrich Holtzmann, a neighbor and carpenter, arrived. He, his wife, and young son lived at the edge of the village on a small plot of the Prince's land.

Seating himself on an overturned basket Ulrich leaned forward and spoke to his friends in a quiet voice, "I have heard of a paper which states many opportunities await one brave enough to travel to Pennsylvania. William Penn promises freedom of religion to all who come. He also holds out the promise of being able to own your own land."

"Penn knows we are good workers and some of the best farmers in Germany. He has made it clear he wants us to come to Penn's Woods, as some call it. He needs good farmers and skilled craftsmen to make his new land prosperous," said Wilhelm who sat next to Peter.

Peter smiled as he added, "I, too, heard all religions are free to come and make Pennsylvania their home."

"William Penn extended that invitation at least thirty years ago," Jakob argued. "Do you think this promise still holds true? Do you think his sons follow his example?"

Wilhelm leaned forward with impatience written on his face, "Look around, Jakob, our land has been ransacked and ruined by the French soldiers. Some have had buildings burned. Families are dying of starvation. Diseases are rampant across the land. Overlords tax us so that we work hard and have nothing in the end. I am willing to take the chance!" With the memory of the afternoon's visit from Overlord Frederich and the soldiers still fresh in his mind Wilhelm couldn't conceal his anger. The tension of the afternoon, spilled out of him into the ears of his friends.

"Your own father was killed by the soldiers, Jakob. Your mother lies ill as we speak," Peter reminded him. His blue eyes shown in the lantern light as he looked directly into Jakob's dark ones.

"You know it is illegal to leave without permission, without paying the necessary fees." Jakob Kramer and his brother, Hans were the best educated of the little group. They were the ones who felt the need to make a good plan before they took action. Jakob's face showed concern, his voice was stern as though he were laying down the rules to a child.

As a young man, Jakob's father had spent several years on the sea. Of the five friends, Jakob and Hans knew best the real dangers of being on the sea. The plan was to go down the Rhine to Rotterdam and then across the sea to Amerika. The Kramer brothers knew the treachery of the Rhine River with its rapids and rocks awaiting the careless sailor.

"My biggest concerns," said Ulrich Holtzmann, "are how much money do we need and who will go. You, Wilhelm, are the oldest one in your family. You and Peter will have to take your younger brothers and sisters with you. I have a wife and a young son. I cannot leave them here."

"We will all go," Peter replied, his determination showing in the set of his jaw as he spoke. "We have been friends since childhood, we will help each other as we always have done. Jakob still has a small scow of his father's that will take us to Rotterdam. When we get there, we will sell it and buy our passage aboard ship. When we get work we will pay Jakob our share of his boat."

"That scow will be too crowded with all of us. That would be more than ten people!" Hans said emphatically. "I fear we will end up in the water!"

Peter spoke up, "Then we will find another way." This was the very attitude that had brought Peter and Wilhelm Meier through many difficult times. Many times they had told each other, "There is always a way through trouble."

Jakob, who never did anything without a complete plan ahead of time, began to calculate aloud. With his eyes on Peter he said, "There will be many fees along the way. We will need food and clothing and supplies. And, I agree, our small boat cannot get us to Rotterdam."

Ulrich, by nature a quiet, logical decision maker, said, "Let us begin now to bring our families into the plan, gathering together all that we can by next Spring. We have nearly six months to get things ready. I think we should leave the area in March, no later than April to go down the Neckar to the Rhine. Wilhelm, when you go down to the river port next week, check on the fees we will need to pay."

Jakob nodded his head in agreement. This seemed to him like a workable beginning, one in which they had time to gather information and adjust accordingly.

They all stood up and began to move toward the door of the shed. Wilhelm motioned his brother to stay behind, as Jakob, Hans, and Ulrich prepared to go out into the night.

When the others were on their way, Wilhelm stood close to Peter and said quietly, "I have been a bit worried over one part of this, Peter. Aside from our brothers and sisters, the only one left in our family is Grandfather Meier. He is too old to make this trip. We cannot leave our younger brothers and sisters here with him, they will have to go with us."

"Katja is nearly seventeen, she will be a help with Daniel and Jorg," Peter responded thoughtfully. "We will all have to help with little Inga. I feel sure mother and father would have approved of our plan, Wilhelm. I am sorry they did not live to hear about it. Perhaps Grandfather can live with his younger sister, Feronica, and her family. Perhaps Feronica's oldest son, Adam, can take over our farm; it would be a better situation for him."

"It is a hard decision. I turn it one way and the other; I am not happy with either way!" Wilhelm said. Then he added, sadly, "We will never see our friends and family again after we leave here." He reflected on the dark side of their decision. "Family is all we have."

Peter could see his brother's body sag with the stress of the idea. "It is the sad part of the adventure," Peter agreed. "But the future is bleak here, also. Pennsylvania looks like a bright spot of hope to me."

"Let us talk to Katja tonight."

"And to Grandfather, too. "

Two

Katja Meier had become the mother of the family after the death of her own mother who succumbed to a combination of starvation and disease, about a year after their father had been killed by French soldiers who had come up from the river looking for food.

Baby Inge had been barely a year old then. The family pulled Inge though that difficult period with milk from their faithful goat, Blume. They survived because they worked together and drew their strength from each other.

Good smells filled the kitchen tonight as the family sat around the long wooden table to a meal of boiled onions and beans with a bit of meat and a few carrots. The boys, Daniel and Jorg, were full of themselves as usual, talking about their day.

"Herr Schwartz gave Daniel a piece of bacon for helping him today. Look! See over there!" Jorg shouted pointing toward the far wall where the bacon hung on a large hook. Herr Schwartz was a neighboring farmer who had three sons, two of whom had gone to Amerika last year. He always looked for extra help especially during harvest and planting time. Twelve year old Daniel, whose face wore a proud smile, felt very good to have earned something to help the family.

Patting Daniel on the shoulder Grandfather said, "You did very well. This spring I think you will be strong enough to hold the plow and help ready the field for planting."

A smile spread over Daniel's face as he filled with pride at Grandfather's compliment.

Peter and Wilhelm looked at each other across the table. They wanted to discuss their plan, but was it safe to do so in front of the younger brothers? Wilhelm decided they must trust them.

Clearing his throat and squaring his shoulders, he said, "Speaking of next spring, Peter and I want to talk with the family about some plans we have been making with Ulrich, Jakob and Hans." He glanced across at Peter, then continued, "We have been told papers were posted in the nearby villages encouraging people to go to America. We think it is time for us to consider such a move."

The family sat quietly for a moment, allowing the reality of the announcement to sink in.

Grandfather turned and looked at Wilhelm in surprise. Katja stared at the two of them not believing her ears. The boys, Daniel and Jorg jumped around in their seats, filled with little boy wiggles of excitement for a new adventure. Immediately the young ones embraced the idea and began laughing and smacking each other on the back, saying, "Ja, Ja, Ja!"

Peter spoke in support of Wilhelm. "We are going to find out what it will cost. The soldiers have ruined our crops several years in a row. The early ice storms of past years hurt our harvest so that we hardly have enough to eat and our seed for planting is limited. It is time to start again with some land of our own!"

At last, Katja found her tongue. "Isn't this very dangerous and expensive? What will happen to us if the two of you leave?" Her pretty face was drawn with concern. She couldn't imagine having to manage alone without these brothers who were the strong dependable part of her life. "You are the ones who have worked the land and taken care of Blume and the pigs and the mule." Katja felt frightened at the prospect of being left here to take care of everything.

Grandfather, who had been sitting quietly, finally said thoughtfully, "Johan Wilhelm, our Prince Elector, proclaimed religious tolerance in the Palatine a few years ago since the churches agreed to pay him a yearly fee." His was the voice of many long years of life when he added, "Even though Lutherans must still be very careful, things are a little better for us now than before. He has not treated us the way the Mennonites or the Huguenots were treated."

"That is true," agreed Katja nodding in agreement, "the

Mennonites were forced to Switzerland." She remembered hugging her friend, Anna Maria, goodbye when that family was forced to leave the area.

Little Inge began to stir, sensing the tension in the conversation even though she didn't really understand it. Katja patted her on the back and gave her a small piece of bread with butter. Inge relaxed under her big sister's touch.

Peter and I think we must take the family -- you, Katja, and Daniel and Jorg and Inge." Then he looked over at Grandfather who sat at the head of table. "Grandfather, you must decide for yourself. You may want to go to your sister, Feronica. Katja is right, the journey will be long and difficult."

"You know you cannot leave without permission and the payment of fees," Grandfather said. His white hair and white beard gave him the appearance of experience and authority.

"Well, that brings us to the next part of the decision," said Peter. He leaned into the table a bit and was very serious. "We agreed that we will not tell anyone of our plans. We will just go when the time comes." He looked at his younger brothers in turn as he said, "Do you hear that Daniel? Do you hear that Jorg?" Peter's face was stern as the two of them wiggled with excitement on their side of the table.

"No matter how excited you feel, you cannot tell your

friends," Peter kept his blue eyes fixed on the two younger brothers. Even the two boys could see their older brothers were quite serious. The youngsters nodded their heads. When Peter and Wilhelm talked like this, they meant it!

"When Papa died, he had three guilders and a few florins hidden away. It was his whole life savings," Katja said. "We still have that, but it will take much more."

She lifted Inge down from her seat at the table so she could move around the room.

Wilhelm said, "Tomorrow I must go to the dock at Mosbach with Overlord Frederich's grain to be sent to market. I will offer myself to work for a day for one of the river boat owners. Peter will go along. Perhaps Daniel and Jorg can go, too. We will not be missed for one day and we should be able to earn some coins toward the trip."

Peter said, "We will go early, boys, and we will be there overnight. We will return day after tomorrow. Katja, you and Grandfather will be safe here for two days."

"I will put some cheese and boiled eggs into a sack for you to take along," Katja said. She was very concerned about the dangers of this new idea with its hope of a new life at the end of the journey.

After everyone was asleep in the sleeping room, Wilhelm still rested by the fire mulling over what lay ahead for the family. As the oldest, he felt responsible for them.

He struggled with his concern as he thought through the difficulties of their plan. Katja, with her beautiful long blond hair and sky blue eyes, had been offered a hand in marriage by several young men on neighboring farms in the past year, but she refused to accept any of them feeling a duty to the family first. Maybe he should have encouraged her to take one of those offers instead of suggesting she go on this dangerous, unpredictable journey. If she waited until she was twenty, she may be too old to marry then what would become of her?

Then there was Grandfather Meier who had quietly asked some very disturbing questions about the journey. He was sixty, getting to be an old man. He had lived on the farm all of his life and had never traveled beyond Heidelberg, let alone to Rotterdam or Amerika! Would he decide to stay with his sister, Feronica, or would he insist on going along? Of course they would not refuse him if he insisted, but the likelihood of his making the voyage successfully was small indeed.

The Meier family had survived by working together and they would continue to do so, no matter what happened to them. Circumstances had made Wilhelm and Peter the father figures, and Katja had become as the mother. They were a close family who helped each other, each doing his part.

Wilhelm could see how this might work. If Grandfather decided to stay here, his sister Feronica's oldest son, Adam, could take over the farm and Grandfather could spend the rest of his days right where he was. Although leaving him behind would be the hardest thing they had ever done.

A last thought frightened Wilhelm. Would Overlord Frederich punish Grandfather for not telling where the family had gone?

Three

Ulrich Holtzmann sat down beside his lovely, dark haired, young wife, Barbara, and their small son. Johannes was just a year old and was already walking across the floor on his strong little legs filling his father's heart with pride and love. Ulrich's heart melted when Johannes said, "Papa."

"Barbara," Ulrich began quietly, "I have been talking with Wilhelm, Peter, Jakob and Hans. We want to make a plan to leave our homeland and find a new life in Amerika." He kept his serious eyes on her face as he spoke. He reached across the table and lay his hand on her arm. As soon as the words fell from his mouth, he felt her shudder slightly.

"Somehow, I knew the five of you were making plans for something. I could tell by the way you talked with each other in whispers," she said looking up at him. "Ulrich, I have heard this is a very dangerous trip!" Her pretty face was filled with a mixture of fear and concern as her eyes searched the face of the tall strong man she loved.

Barbara rose from the table and picked up Johannes placing him in his small chair at his spot by the table. She was the third daughter of a poor local farmer, who like Wilhelm Meier, worked the land for a rich landowner but owned nothing himself. Like Wilhelm, Peter, and other poor farmers, no one in her family could read or write.

Ulrich watched her taking care of Johannes. "I know you are worried, Barbara, but we must focus on our future. This is our hope for a better life." Ulrich continued, trying to calm Barbara's fears. "We have some coins saved, but we will need many more before we arrive in Philadelphia. When we get there we will have the freedom to own land and someday I can have a carpenter business of my own. Our son will be able to have a true education and the freedom to be what he wants to be."

Barbara leaned over the kettle in the fireplace and put some spatzle on Johannes' plate which she placed in front of him. Johannes wiggled with delight stuffing the spatzle in his mouth with his fingers. It was his favorite food. "Gut, Mama," he uttered through the mouthful.

Like other wives, Barbara usually followed her husband's decisions with little resistance. She said, "Do you think you can be paid in coin for your next job?"

Sometimes Ulrich was paid for his work in coin, sometimes in goods. Because he was a carpenter, he was good with numbers. From his own father he learned to read and write enough to take care of his business needs. He could write his name and the words necessary for his work.

Like Grandfather Meier, Barbara had never been far from home. The thought of leaving her family and all that was familiar frightened her. She looked across the table at him, "I am afraid, Ulrich. What if something happens to one of us on the way? The people at church say the journey is very long and difficult. They say only fools do this!"

Barbara sat a bowl of spatzle and bread before her husband.

"We must have faith, Barbara. Things happen right here. Please, begin to plan what we should take. Space will very limited on board. I must take some of my carpenter tools. We will need extra clothes and coats. I will make one trunk to contain everything."

Surrendering to the idea, she began to think what they would need. "I will dry apples for us," she said, "and save some grain. I can make extra cheese, and dried peas and beans."

She asked, "When will we be leaving?" Her eyes wandered around the room, already assessing what could go and what would have to stay. It was more than a little unnerving to think of leaving all that was familiar.

"Right now we are planning to go in Spring, probably March. It takes weeks, maybe months to make the trip. With real luck, maybe we could be there by the end of July."

They ate the rest of their spatzle and bread in silence, each thinking about the plan to find a new life. It was thrilling, inspiring, and terribly formidable.

Finally, Barbara broke the silence. With some uneasiness she said, "What do you think I should tell my mother and father?" She wiped the butter and noodles from Johannes' face and lifted him down from the table.

"Unfortunately, I must ask you to say nothing. You know we must have permission and pay fees to the magistrates. We must not discuss this with anyone right now. It would just make things difficult."

Then a thought struck Barbara, "Ulrich, what will Jakob do with his sick mother? Who will take care of his younger brother, Hans?" The serious implications of this plan were beginning to trouble her.

"Hans can choose to go with us or stay here and run the shop. He is eighteen. By March he will be nineteen. He is a man and certainly old enough to make such a choice. As for Jakob's mother, we will wait and see. She is extremely ill."

Ulrich had given thought to the money problem. He began to explain to Barbara, "Tomorrow, I start the new work shed at Gerber's. I will ask him to pay me in coin -- at least in part. I dare not act too anxious about it, but I will tell him I have a debt I need to pay. I say this just in case you are talking to his wife at the leather shop or at church."

He knew that in this little village news traveled quickly. Many people bartered when he did work for them because they had few coins. Now he would have to try to get them to pay using their limited cash without making them suspicious.

A hour had passed and Ulrich picked up his small, happy son from the rug in front of the fireplace. Johannes reached for the little toy dog his mother had made for him out of a rabbit skin stuffed with straw. He always slept with Hund. Ulrich sang to him as he carried him to his bed in the sleeping room. Sometimes he told Johannes stories but tonight he had too much on his mind. He never read to him, for there were no books in the house.

Ulrich tried not to worry Barbara, but he knew the dangers of the plan; however he believed in himself. He thought: if I take some of my best tools I should find work quickly. After all, I am from a long line of carpenters and builders. Surely a place like Pennsylvania needs good carpenters.

He and Barbara sat quietly by the fire for a little while after Johannes had gone to sleep. Barbara said, "At church I heard that some people, who lived southwest of here, went to a place called Lancaster Plain a few years ago. The ladies at church thought they were Mennonites who had run away from Switzerland as a group."

They sat close, near the warming fire enjoying the comfort of each other. "I have heard of several of those groups," he said, "One in 1710 and another a few years later."

"It would be easier to go in a group," Barbara said, almost to herself.

"We are in a group. We are with friends." Ulrich could feel her body relax a little against him. "In the village I heard about some others who had lived in Waldangeloch. They went to a small village west of Philadelphia called Germantown."

Finally, they retired to the sleeping room themselves, Ulrich lay beside her trying to calm his own fears. He didn't know exactly where Chester or Lancaster Plain or Germantown were, but he was sure he could find his way. If others could do it, so could he.

Four

JAKOB KRAMER'S NEIGHBOR, OLD Frau Gartner, did the cooking and cleaning for 'the boys' as she called them. She had the stew warming in the fireplace when Jakob came into the house.

A smile crossed his face as soon as the good aromas reached his nose. "Ummmmm. Gut riechen!" he said sniffing the air. Then he noticed the serious expression on Old Frau's face.

"Jakob, I have tried all day to get your mother to eat," she commented softly. "I have not been successful as you can see, and I am very concerned about her."

Jakob's smile faded as he listened to her report. She took very good care of Mama. She was a good hearted woman whom he trusted. "I know it gets more difficult each day. You do a good job with her, Frau. She likes having you here."

Jakob allowed Frau to take home food and supplies to Herr

Gartner who could no longer walk well enough to do much work. She was kind and dependable. The arrangement worked out very well.

Jakob took Mother's bowl of stew from Frau's hand and walked over to his mother. She was sitting quietly on her chair near the warm fireplace. Frau had mashed the vegetables in Mother's stew so that it was nearly drinkable, almost porridge-like. As most of the people in their late forties, she had very few teeth. He spoke to her quietly, "I have your supper, Mama."

Very ill and quite frail, she opened her eyes when she heard her son's voice. For a fleeting moment she saw him in her mind as the boy he used to be. Jakob had been so cute with his dark curls and dark eyes, so different from his light-hearted, fair-haired little brother.

"Eat a little of this, Mama," he coaxed. She tried to swallow a little of it as he gently held the bowl to her mouth. Her throat was so sore she could hardly swallow, her chest was tight, and breathing was painful and difficult. She kept a smile on her face, but she knew she was getting weaker each day.

Finally she leaned back on her chair and closed her eyes, "That is enough, Jakob." She sighed, everything was too much effort; she felt exhausted. Even with Jakob's coaxing she could eat no more.

She knew Jakob would take care of everyone. He had always been the serious one, clever and quick thinking. She remembered how he saved his little brother when the

French soldiers looted the shop and killed his father. She trembled a bit as she remembered the terrible scene.

Jakob could not know what she was thinking, but he saw the shudder and stroked her arms in a comforting gentle way, as one would do with a child.

The wind swept into the room as the door opened and Hans came in from outside, shaking the rain from his clothing and boots. He hung his wet coat on the wall peg. "I bought some pottery today from Herr Fritz. I managed to get it to the store without breaking a single piece!" He smiled at his brother. Then quietly went over and kissed his mother lightly on the cheek, "How goes it Mama?" He squeezed her hand gently.

She didn't answer him, her eyes closed. She felt as though her strength was gone.

Jakob and Hans Kramer were shopkeepers in the small village. They sold things made by the farmers and craftsmen to people in the other villages, to the people at the church, and to travelers who came by on their way to Heidelberg. Their father had been a shopkeeper and his father before him. They were descended from a long line of them.

"How much did you pay him?" asked Jakob, sitting down to the table.

"Oh, I made a good bargain. He wanted some of Herr Gerber's leather harness. I just happened to have some in the wagon, so we made a trade."

"You are good, Hans!" Jakob teased his eighteen year old brother. "I have taught you well!" It was no surprise to Jakob that Hans had made a good trade. "You have a natural talent for working with people." Jakob's eyes rested on his brother, appreciating the handsome, light-hearted, chatty person he was.

Both Hans and Jakob were good with figures and could do them quickly in their heads. Their father had taught them to read and write. It was necessary for running the shop.

Hans continued commenting on the daily events as he sat down to the table with Jakob. "I stopped at the tinsmith and the shoemaker today, to see what they may have for us. You know how they are! They know all the gossip." He grinned.

Hans loved finding out the news. "The tinsmith said there was a shoemaker from Erfurt who went to a place called Chester, in Pennsylvania."

Jakob made no reply. He just looked at Hans trying to read his thoughts on travelling to Amerika. He didn't want to discuss this subject until Frau had gone home.

Frau Gartner gently took Mama into the sleeping room. When she had made her comfortable on the sleeping mat, she covered her with a quilt, patted her arm, and left her to rest. "You sleep now, and I will see you in the morning."

She filled two bowls with stew for the brothers, put the bread on the table, and then got ready to go out into the rain, taking her tin of stew with her. "I'll see you in the morning," she said trying not to show the sadness she felt for their mother whose situation was grim. She pulled her coat around her and opened the door to the wind and rain.

Frau had seen many die of this congestive disease -- mostly the older ones and the very young. She thought to herself, I would never mention it to the boys, but I know there is no cure. I know the end is near for their dear mother.

As Hans and Jakob began their meal, Jakob said, "Hans, what do you think about our plans? the risks? the benefits?"

Hans stopped eating, a generous chunk of bread midway to his mouth, and studied his brother. He said, "I noticed that you were not as excited as Wilhelm and Peter last night, but I equated it to your serious way of thinking."

"I want to go, of course!" Hans answered the question. He had been for the idea immediately as he was younger and never thought of danger. "I think it is a wonderful opportunity." He added, "How long do you think this will take? When will we leave? What do you think it will cost?"

"I would think several weeks from Heidelberg to Rotterdam, then on to Philadelphia, stopping along the way in England maybe. I expect at least three months, maybe more, depending on the winds and the weather," Jakob answered.

"From the beginning the whole idea is exciting to me!" Hans was enthusiastic. "I dreamed of this, but I never thought it would come true!"

"It is very expensive," Jakob continued soberly. "I worry that Wilhelm and Peter may have to find someone in Amerika to redeem them from the ship and pay their fees. But then… they have nothing here."

Hans looked thoughtful; he was beginning to see problems which he hadn't considered. "Well, Ulrich may be able to save enough because sometimes he gets paid in coin. We have always kept some coins hidden and could save a bit more if we worked on it. Our finances are the best of the group."

Then another thought struck Hans. He sat up straight, his blue eyes fixed on Jakob's dark ones. "We cannot just walk away from the store! People depend on us. What will we do?"

"We need to plan. Think about it Hans. Let me know your ideas. We must be careful how we handle our departure."

The shop had been in their family for generations. If they just walked away from it, they had much to lose. The Kramer's shop and house was not the two-room style of the farmers, instead it had two additional rooms upstairs over the store. It was located near the center of the small village. It had a tiny yard with a small garden. For this privilege Jakob paid high taxes to the owner of the village.

The brothers continued to talk about what needed to be done as they finished their stew. They banked the fire for the night, then checked on Mama. She seemed to be resting, so they went to their sleeping room, too. It had been a long busy day.

Tired as he was, sleep didn't come quickly to Jakob as he lay on his bed, thinking about Hans. "If I didn't go, there would easily be enough money for Hans. I could join him in another year or two. We will decide later; we have so much planning to do in the next few months." And he closed his eyes on that last thought.

Five

EARLY THE NEXT MORNING Wilhelm, Peter, Daniel, and Jorg loaded the wagon with Overlord Frederich's grain and started for the market on the Neckar River near Mosbach. Before noon, they reached the destination where their overlord had directed them to deliver the grain to a certain dealer. After they finished unloading it, they ate the food Katja had fixed for them. Looking for extra work they went to the river dock where there were boat captains looking for men to hire.

It wasn't long until they found Captain Jager, owner of a medium sized craft, looking for extra help. "Are you looking for work, fellows? I need some men to load all the goods from the warehouse across the road onto the boat. I will be going to Heidelberg and then down the Rhine to Koln with some of this cargo."

The Meiers jumped at the chance and followed him to the building. "When it is dusk," the Captain said, "come to the storage building and I will give you something to eat.

Tomorrow, I have a few more things in a second building to load."

They worked the rest of the afternoon. At dusk, they found the captain. "We have finished all that you gave us to load, Sir," Wilhelm said, hoping the captain would remember about the supper for they had brought no money with which to buy an evening meal.

This captain was better than most; he motioned to the bread and the tin of cold soup on the table. Smiling at his young workers Captain Jager said, "Be back at dawn tomorrow. You can sleep in the stable where you put the mule and cart." He was to give them two shillings when the loading was finished.

Early the next morning the four of them returned to dock and Captain Jager's boat. The captain showed them the storage building which contained woven materials and carved wooden figures to be loaded.

They were finished before noon. The Captain gave the shillings to Wilhelm who pushed the coins deep into the purse under his shirt where they would be safe. "Thank you, Sir."

The older brothers knew that at this rate, they may be able to afford passage for Katja and Inge but the rest of them may have to find a sponsor to redeem their debt.

"Let's walk around the marketplace and see what we can learn," Peter suggested. "Meet at the wagon by mid afternoon. Daniel, you and Jorg stay together, so you don't get lost."

Heading off in his own direction, Peter was drawn to a well-dressed man near the town fountain talking about Pennsylvania. He walked over to listen to him.

A large crowd of men gathered around the speaker who was a lively, animated fellow with a thick head of blonde hair done in a neat coiffure. "There is so much money to be made in the new land," the man was telling the crowd. He showed off his fine clothes, stroking them with his hand, and told them, "I am able to afford these fine things because I became so rich in Amerika. I have made a fortune."

He looked at his audience of poor farmers and workers, "Sign up with me, and I will take care of you for the entire trip. It will only cost you only two guilders. That is a better price than others will charge you."

Peter carefully observed this man, who called himself Mr. Wells. He was certainly well dressed, in a new woolen coat and fine leather shoes.

Peter was not educated, but he suspected what the man was saying was not quite true. However, he did keep the paper the man shoved into everyone's hands. He would have Jakob read it to them next time they got together. He stuck it safely down in his purse under his shirt. He kept to the edge of the crowd and listened while some of the others asked more questions about the trip and the fees.

Wells' gaze fell on handsome, strong looking Peter. "You there, young fellow, how about signing up. A good job will be waiting on the other side of the ocean for a fellow like you. Just put your mark on this paper. You will never get a better offer for just two guilders!"

Peter shook his head, but did not say anything. He did notice a few men who seemed to be considering the offer As they talked among themselves, Peter could hear their conversation: "This sounds like a good price." and "If we did this, we could save money and bring our families later."

Mr. Wells told them to bring their two guilders to him in the morning and they would be on their way to riches.

❀   ❀   ❀

Meanwhile, Daniel and Jorg went back to the captain who had hired them. "Do you ever hire people to help you on the boat when you sail to Rotterdam?" Daniel asked.

Wide-eyed with surprise at Daniel's question, Jorg's expression sent a warning look to his brother.

Captain Jager looked down at the young face questioning him. "Are you thinking of going to Rotterdam, Son?" he asked, for he had not missed Jorg's warning glance.

"Well… no…not right now. Maybe someday I will," Daniel replied, realizing he had gotten in too deeply too soon, and he had read Jorg's warning clearly. Wilhelm and Peter told him this was a secret.

Captain Jager's gaze remained on the boy with the intelligent, inquisitive mind who made him think of his own son whom he had lost to smallpox about a year ago. He instantly liked these two young boys and almost wished they were his. He smiled and pretended to believe Daniel. He thought to himself, lately there are more and more of these poor farmers trying to find a way to Rotterdam.

"Sometimes I hire fellows to help me," Captain Jager said. He put his hand on Daniel's shoulder. "Just be very careful who you believe, Son. Not all people you meet here at the river port are honest."

❀   ❀   ❀

Wilhelm went back the stable where they had put the wagon and drew two bags from under the seat. One was a bag of grain he had hidden away to barter for some material for Katja to make a new dress or two. He walked to the end of the row of merchants where he found a weaver with his colorful materials spread out on the table in front of him. "How much material can I get in trade for this bag of grain?" he asked, holding the bag out to the merchant.

The weaver took the sack and looked inside. Putting his hand in it, he allowed the grain to fall through his fingers. It was fresh and good, not wet or infested with insects. He smiled, and thought how happy his wife would be with something so fresh and good as this. He could almost smell the loaves of fresh bread that this would make. Maybe there would even be enough for his favorite cake. Careful not to appear too interested, he made his voice sound gruff, "Enough for one dress."

Wilhelm frowned, "This grain is fresh and clean. I think maybe enough for two dresses would be a fair trade."

The weaver had expected this. Grain like this would make his wife so happy, he should trade it for material for three dresses, but he said gruffly, "Ok. Two dresses, that is all!"

Wilhelm smiled, "Wonderful! I'll take it." He picked two different colors, a deep blue and a color like red wine. Katja would be delighted. She was such a good sister who worked very hard for the family without ever complaining. She deserved this little treat.

The weaver rolled up the cloth and tied it with a cord. "I hope your wife likes your choices, Son."

"I am sure she will," Wilhelm smiled. Of course the weaver didn't know he didn't have a wife!

Wilhelm took the other sack to the shoemaker. There he wanted to trade the fresh goat cheese and the bag of dried peas and beans for a pair of shoes for Daniel who was growing so fast he had to give his old shoes to Jorg.

As he walked into the shop, the shoemaker noticed Wilhelm's big, poorly shod feet. He started to say, he didn't have anything that size.

"I want them for a young boy who will wear them a year I hope." Wilhelm interrupted.

The shoemaker pulled a pair from under his table. This was the only extra pair the shoemaker had ready for sale. Usually people ordered their shoes; he made them in the next week or so. Now and then he had a bit of leather left over and made an extra pair. "You are very lucky today," the shoemaker said. "The butcher paid me with extra leather when I made his new shoes! It is good leather. He tanned it himself. These will last a boy a long time."

Looking at the sun to estimate the time and feeling happy with his purchases, Wilhelm hurried toward the wagon stopping briefly at the Lutheran church to speak with the only man he really trusted in Mosbach.

Approaching the Reverend, he greeted him fondly and said, "Sir I need to ask you a question in confidence."

"Certainly, go ahead, Wilhelm, what can I do for you?"

"Sir, do you know anything about the amount of money needed to pay for travel on the river to Rotterdam and then to Amerika?"

"Come walk with me, Son, away from this crowd of ears," the old Father said, taking Wilhelm by the arm as though he were going to counsel him privately on a pressing spiritual problem.

Wilhelm trusted Father Josef because he had been a friend of his own father long ago before the French soldiers had come. The old Reverend said, "Wilhelm, be very careful when you speak of this. You know if Overlord Frederich, or any of the Prince's soldiers hear, you will be punished. Other people who hear you speak of it, may turn you in for a reward or to win favor with the Prince Elector. It is very dangerous to speak carelessly of such plans."

"I know. It is why I dared only to come to you," Wilhelm looked at the old reverend.

"I know you will have to pay a toll to every little castle tyrant along the river from Bingen to the Dutch border. There are more than thirty of them." The reverend kept his eyes on Wilhelm to see how this information was effecting him. "I know also that you will have to take food to eat on the river and maybe to hold you over at Rotterdam for a week. You may be able to find a little work loading ships. These things I know for sure."

Wilhelm heard these words with a heavy heart for this confirmed the difficulty of their plan. It suddenly seemed like so much responsibility was resting on his shoulders. For the first time, the idea seemed daunting.

The trusted old friend continued, "I understand that the ships go from Rotterdam to Cowes or sometimes to Liverpool to pick up more cargo. Again, you may wait there, maybe for several days or weeks. Then, the trip across the sea takes about eight weeks, if the weather is agreeable. It could take two or three months or more under the worst conditions."

The old man continued to keep his eyes fixed on the oldest son of his good friend. He continued, "Use a good sturdy trunk for your belongings and keep a sharp eye on it. Never let it out of your sight! There are plenty of thieves in all these places. I have even heard you cannot trust some of the ship's masters!"

The Reverend's heart went out to this poor farmer who owned nothing -- not the land he worked nor the house he lived in. But the Reverend also knew Wilhelm was a good man who worked hard to take care of his brothers and sisters after the deaths of the parents. "Wilhelm, you will need at least four, maybe more, guilders for every adult, and that doesn't include the trip down the Rhine or costs of waiting in Rotterdam or Cowes."

"That is so much money," Wilhelm said softly, his heart sinking with despair.

"Whatever money you have, Wilhelm, keep it hidden in a safe place. Don't let people see where it is kept. Don't keep all your money in the same place."

Father Josef reached down into the purse hidden in his robes. Handing Wilhelm two coins, he said, "I wish I could help you more, but we all have so little these days. Take these two coins in memory of my old friend, your father. Remember what I have told you. Be very careful about trusting people you do not know."

Wilhelm looked down at the coins and smiled at the old man. "Thank you so much, Father Josef. You have always been a good friend. My father is surely smiling on you from Heaven."

To himself, he thought, four or more guilders for each adult! That is a fortune! Wilhelm had never seen that much money, let alone, dreamt of having that much!

Six

WILHELM AND HIS BROTHERS arrived home just before the evening meal. Katja and little Inge came out to greet them, glad they were home safely. Inge jumped on Daniel's back for a horse ride around the house and through the door into the cooking room.

Katja had schnitz and knepp ready for supper. Good smells filled the room as they all sat down at the long table to talk about their day. Daniel and Jorg dug into their dumplings as though they were starved.

"Haven't you two eaten since you left two days ago!" Grandfather laughed.

Wilhelm couldn't wait to give Katja the material he had bartered for her. Drawing it from behind his back, he said casually, "Oh, look what I found at the marketplace in Mosbach!" He handed it across the table to her.

Katja's eyes grew wide. When she caught sight of the colorful materials, a smile spread over her pretty face. "Oh, Wilhelm, how did you do this?" she exclaimed as she ran her hand over the material. It was smooth and soft. "You picked my favorite blue! And, the wine color will look beautiful with the little bit of white material I have from before!"

She held the material out to Inge, "Look, Little One, I can make this go far enough so that I will have something for you, too!"

Even little girls of two years understand the joy of a new dress. Inge laughed out loud with delight and clapped her hands.

Wilhelm grinned, "Overlord Frederich will never notice there was one a small bag of grain less when they weighed it at the Waage Haus."

"That is very dangerous, Wilhelm," cautioned Grandfather. He sounded stern, but the twinkle in his eye belied the seriousness of the words. They all got a little satisfaction out of taking just a bit from the man who took everything he could from them.

Peter pulled out the paper he got from the Newlander. "I listened to this man speak. He shoved one these papers into my hand. He says he can get us to Amerika for two guilders, and he will take care of everything!" He handed the paper across the table to Wilhelm and Grandfather, but since none of them could read, they did not really know what it said.

Wilhelm pushed the paper away. "Oh, Peter! First of all, if

anyone saw you standing there taking that fellow's papers he will report us! Father Josef told me not to trust these Newlanders. They are trying to trick you. They get paid for getting you on board; they do nothing but steal your money. The captain will sell you for years of service to anyone who will pay your fees!"

"He was dressed in very nice clothing, and he said he made a fortune in Amerika! Several people in the group were going to sign up with him!" Peter insisted. He felt a bit indignant at Wilhelm's suggestion that he was taken in by the Newlander, Mr. Wells.

"Father Josef said these Newlanders have never been to Amerika. They are crooks!" Wilhelm argued. "Father Josef said it costs at least four guilders for every adult. Daniel and Jorg may be a bit less." Wilhelm couldn't bring himself to say the words " it could be more." He just had to hope it would not be that much.

The family looked at him saying nothing as this news settled into their minds. Katja looked across the table at her brothers. Maybe this is just a dream that can't come true, she thought sadly. Who had that kind of money?

Wilhelm continued, "Father Josef also said there is a fee for every land owner along the Rhine. And, we must be prepared to wait in Rotterdam and again in England."

"That is a lot of money!" Grandfather exclaimed. "I think in my whole life, I have never had that much money all at one time!" The family nodded their heads in agreement.

It was true; they never had more than a guilder or so at once.

"Let me tell you what Jorg and I did this afternoon!" Daniel told of his conversation with Captain Jager. "Do you think he could take us part way, and we could earn a little money by helping him? I liked him, and I think he is honest."

"He liked us!" Jorg added, happy to help Daniel tell the tale. "He said we should be careful and not trust everyone we see on the dock."

Grandfather turned to Jorg, "That is good advice, Kinder, keep it in mind when you are in the village."

Peter considered Daniel's idea. "You may have something there, Daniel. We will work on that. It would help him and us."

Daniel and Jorg smacked each other on the back, "Ja!"

"We can talk to Jakob and see what he thinks." Wilhelm trusted Jakob's judgment above all the others because Jakob was more experienced and he was educated.

"There is one more thing," Wilhelm added mysteriously. He got up from the table and walked outside the door. He picked up the new shoes, hiding them behind his back as he returned to the table. "The shoemaker had an extra pair, and I traded for some fresh goat cheese and a bag of dried peas and beans." He pulled the shoes out and put them in front of Daniel. "At least you will not go to Amerika barefooted!"

Daniel jumped up and gave a yelp of delight. "Wonderful, wonderful!" he said, slipping his feet into them. "I don't think I've ever had a never-worn, *new* pair of shoes! Wonderful! Wonderful!" and he danced around the room in delight.

His little boy heart could not have been happier with a million guilders!

Seven

ULRICH AND TWO OTHER men, who were Herr Gerber's neighbors, gathered early in the morning to begin work on Gerber's new shed. Herr Gerber was a tanner and leather worker who sold his best leather to shoemakers and made harness and work pieces with the rest. Because his old shed was in bad condition, he decided a new one was needed with better, dryer places to store his materials.

"Here is the plan," Herr Gerber told Ulrich and the two others. "Take the old shed down; use whatever lumber we can from the old one to frame out the new one. Using the best parts of the old will save quite a bit of expense. The outside is worse than the inside; the big oak rafters are still good and can be reused."

It didn't take long to tear down the old shed and decide which pieces could still be used. The men chatted about the weather, their families, and their neighbors as they hammered and cut. Nothing was wasted. The surrounding mountains made getting more lumber easy. By the end of the afternoon they had the framework ready and would probably finish within the next day or two if the weather held.

Ulrich drew Herr Gerber over to the side at the end of the day and spoke quietly with him, "I wanted to ask you if you could pay some of what you owe me in coin. I know that is hard for you, so I will be happy to barter for part of it. I have some debt I am pressured to pay."

Herr Gerber, an older man than Ulrich, gave him a long searching look. He suspected this was not the exact truth. He stroked his dark curly beard with his stocky muscular hands and thought about whether to question Ulrich further. Finally he answered, "I will do what I can, Ulrich." He walked away thinking that was a very strange request, one he had never heard Ulrich make before. "I wonder… something is going on," he murmured to himself.

❀   ❀   ❀

The next morning, Samuel, one of the neighbors who had come to help had a paper his cousin had given him almost two weeks ago. Holding it out toward them, he said, "Klaus brought this home from Heidelberg. Klaus told us he listened to this man speaking to a group of people trying to get them to sign up to go to Amerika. Have you ever heard of this?" Samuel looked at the workers who stood around him.

"What did the man say?" asked Heinrich, the other worker.

"My cousin, Klaus, said he wanted people to go with him to Amerika. He said it would only cost two pounds English or two guilders. He wanted them to sign up right then and there." Samuel was obviously very impressed that anyone would decide something that serious so quickly.

"Did Klaus do it?" asked Ulrich trying to show only casual interest.

"Well, cousin Klaus didn't. But his friend Karl did; so did Karl's brother! They are going to leave this week!" Samuel seemed pleased relay this gossip.

"Could he read the paper he made his mark upon?" Ulrich wondered aloud.

"No."

"Then how did he know what he was signing?" asked Heinrich, amazed. Neither he nor Samuel could read, and he knew *he* would never sign anything like that.

Samuel shrugged his shoulders. "The man who was speaking told him it was fine. He told them it just said he would take them to Amerika. He said many men have done this, and now they are rich and wear fine clothes just like he does."

"I saw one of those papers at the church several weeks ago," Heinrich said thinking about his experience with this. "One man who could read a little, said the paper stated at the end of the voyage you will still owe some money."

Heinrich's face showed his puzzlement over the difference between the stories.

"Did Klaus say anything about other costs to get to Rotterdam?" Ulrich asked Samuel, pressing for a bit more information. He remembered Wilhelm's conversation with Father Josef.

"No," Samuel waved away the question, "The man in Heidelberg just said he would take them if they signed right away."

Ulrich was not convinced, "That sounds too good to be true! The 'right away' part really bothers me." He realized that Klaus had been talking to a Newlander like the ones Father Josef had warned Wilhelm about. "Klaus should be careful. Some of these fellows are just crooks who take your money."

Ulrich reached out his hand, "Let me see your paper, Samuel."

He looked down at the paper. He could not read well enough to understand every word of it. It seemed to be a letter from someone north of Heidelberg near Erfurt.

He read what he could to the men. "It seems like a letter. The writer says he went to Amerika last year and is sending this letter back home to his father and mother. He is doing well and has work. He writes, *I am making so much money in Amerika I am going to buy some land next year.*" Ulrich lifted his eyes from the paper to the listeners. "I cannot read every word."

Samuel told them, "The agreement that Klaus's friend Karl signed was in English. Karl cannot read German, and he certainly cannot read English!"

"Are they taking their families?" asked Heinrich.

"Karl and his brother have no families. They are just two young men eighteen years and twenty years. They will go by themselves."

By nightfall, the shed was almost finished and Ulrich started home to his wife and son. At supper, he told Barbara about the day's conversation.

"We must save as much money as we can," he said. "I do not think it is safe or wise to listen to these men who talk you into signing papers right away; especially papers that you do not understand. We must be very careful and plan well before we do this."

He put his arm around Johannes who snuggled his little body against Papa. Ulrich desperately wanted something better for his son, but he didn't want to put him in danger.

"We still have a few months to prepare," Barbara said. "I have been working to dry some fruits and peas and beans. And I have been making some goat cheese to take along for Johannes, for he will not get the good goat's milk on the ship."

Ulrich smiled across the table at his lovely wife. "We will have to put a coat and some blankets in the trunk.

It sounds like we will need them on the way. And, I have been thinking, whatever tools I cannot take in the trunk, I will leave for your brother, Krischian. But we cannot tell him now."

After Johannes was sound asleep, Barbara and Ulrich lay on their sleeping mat talking into the night, planning what to take. Finally, they fell asleep still trying to figure out how to get their whole lives in just one trunk.

Eight

OLD FRAU GARTNER TOLD Jakob and Hans their mother was getting weaker every day. "Today I could not get her to eat anything at all. She just slept all day." Frau was obviously upset to have to say this to the boys for she could see the end was near. "Prepare yourselves," she counseled them sadly, "for I have seen many situations like this in the past few years. It is a disease that wears them out just trying to breathe! "

That night Hans and Jakob took turns sitting up with their mother, but by morning it was clear they would lose her very soon. Hans walked to the Lutheran Church to ask the Reverend to come to the house.

A day later, they laid their mother to rest in the church yard beside her husband, their father, also named Jakob. Jakob and Hans were well known in the village and many people came to give their condolences to the family. A few people brought a small token gift of remembrance which the boys put carefully away.

That evening as they sat eating the bread and sausage prepared for them by Frau Gartner, Hans said sadly, "We knew this would happen. I try to think that at least she is spared the harshness of the times we face. She is at peace and with Papa."

❀   ❀   ❀

As the two of them worked in the shop the next day, they talked of their plans between customers. "Hans, if I stay here, we will easily have enough money for you to go to Amerika. You go first and I will come later, after you get settled."

"No, Jakob," Hans countered. "You have no reason to stay here now. Mama and Papa are both gone. It is just you and me. We have enough money to take care of the two of us. We will stay together. We will make it. We have always worked together and helped each other. It will be as always. I could not go without you and let you to face the wrath of Overlord Frederich and the Prince when they find we are missing."

"Be reasonable, Hans." Jakob continued to argue, looking authoritatively at his younger brother. "We will need at least ten, maybe twenty, guilders for the two of us to get started in a shop in Amerika."

"If we save everything we make for the next two or three months and sell some of our things, we can do it and even have money to spare. We are much better off than Wilhelm and better than even Ulrich," Hans pointed out. "There are only two of us. Think of Wilhelm. There are six of them, plus Grandfather!"

But Jakob, the serious one, was not completely convinced. He was still solving every possible problem. "What will we do with the shop? It is the only one in the village. People depend on us to sell their goods."

"I have been thinking about that," Hans replied.

But just then the wife of the blacksmith came into the shop. She greeted them pleasantly, "Good Morning, Gentlemen. Do you have some good cheese this morning?"

Jakob hurried off to get the kind he knew was her favorite. "We know the kind you like, Frau Schmidt, right from the farm of Herr Baum." He smiled as he cut her a nice chunk. Off she went happily -- as always.

When Frau Schmidt was a little way down the street, Hans said "I wonder if Old Frau's grandson, Lukas, would be interested in running the shop for us. He does well when he comes in to help us. We will go on a trip to Heidelberg, and when we don't come back it will be his. He will honestly not know anything about the plan."

"Yes, he has worked for us before and did very well," Jakob agreed nodding his head. He added, "We will have to be very careful when we ask him; he has always shown himself to be honest and does not indulge in the town gossip. We should see what he thinks. Tomorrow I will discuss it with him."

"I heard Lukas was thinking of marrying. I think he has his eye on that pretty Maria Rauscherin. This opportunity would certainly make that a possibility! A full purse would make him much more handsome!" laughed Hans.

❁   ❁   ❁

The next day, Jakob asked Lukas to come to the shop. The two of them went back to the cooking room table so they could sit down and talk privately. Jakob said, "We decided to find an apprentice, Lukas. We wanted to see if you are interested since you've worked with us before."

"Yes, I do want more work. I am planning to get married, you know," Lukas smiled proudly. "I am interested in being an apprentice so that I could learn to run a shop of my own."

He happily agreed to take some food as payment plus a small amount of cash for his work while he was learning how to keep the shop stocked with goods people wanted and how to balance the accounts. He had helped out many times, so he already knew a lot about how the little shop was operated. Lucas knew how to read and write, too, thanks to one of the local priests who had taken an interest in educating some of the village boys.

"You come in as an apprentice tomorrow, Lukas," Jakob said trying to sound very businesslike so as avoid any suspicion. He thought to himself, now we have several months to get Lukas prepared.

Jakob hadn't said anything about leaving the area, but he thought Lukas sensed the truth. He knew he was glad for the opportunity.

❁   ❁   ❁

Frau Gartner was very pleased that Jakob and Hans had taken Lukas under their wing, for he was twenty years and he had many younger brothers. Old Frau, herself, had her own thoughts about why Jakob and Hans were employing him. Of this she said nothing, not even to Lukas. Old Frau would never be the one to tell what she knew about the two young men who had been so helpful to her and her husband in their old age.

She thought to herself, "I noticed the new trunk covered with a cloth to look like a table in the corner of the upstairs room. Jakob and Hans had put blankets and coats and two pairs of new pants in their room. Now I understand why!"

Old Frau had lived in this village, in the small house next to the Kramer family for her entire life. She knew everything about everyone.

Nine

THE FOLLOWING MORNING AFTER getting Lukas settled, the two brothers hitched up the old horse and started off to visit the neighboring farmers and skilled craftsmen.

Having Lukas there allowed Jakob and Hans to go together to barter for cheeses and dried goods to sell in the shop. It gave them time and a safe place to talk privately and do some planning. They put some of their goods away in storage in preparation for the trip.

Business was good today. The blacksmith had some tools he had made to sell in their shop. He had a daughter who was getting married soon to the weaver's son, and he wanted to be able to have a big wedding dinner and a nice gift for the new bride.

The shoemaker had two new pairs of shoes for ladies made of good goat skin. He also had a lot of gossip about how the soldiers were listening to tales being told by people who were trying gain favor with the Prince Elector. The shoemaker told them, "You can never trust anyone, boys. People will do anything to make themselves look good!"

By afternoon, Hans and Jakob had traded for several kinds of cheese from neighboring farmers, and knowing they had made good bargains, turned back toward the village. "It was a good day, Hans," smiled Jakob, clucking the old horse into a trot.

The road before them was lined with pines that created a pleasant ride as faithful old Rostig pulled them homeward. Just as the two brothers began to relax, they heard the heavy gallop of a large horse behind them. They turned to see an approaching horse and rider. The Prince's soldier rode to the front of the wagon and stopped them.

"I have noticed that you are gathering a lot of cheeses and goods for your shop, Jakob. Is business that good?" This one, like all the Prince's soldiers, was overbearing and surly, quick to cause trouble. He frowned down at them from his horse.

Although he felt anything but calm, Jakob kept his voice steady, "Winter is near, and people need extra food to keep well, Sir. Cheese is a good thing. It is healthy, and one does not need to waste wood cooking it."

The soldier didn't smile, but kept his eyes on Jakob and his hand on his sword, trying to frighten him into saying something he would regret later. He was quite menacing as he looked down from the back of his huge black horse. His dragoon uniform with its military design communicated a threatening air of authority.

Neither brother dared to irritate this man. Hans reached into one of the containers in the wagon. "Surely your children like cheese, Sir?" Hans asked, smiling as he held out a nice sized piece for the soldier to take with him. "This is from one of our best cheese makers. We just got it this afternoon. It is fresh and good!"

The man looked down at Hans. He hesitated as though he were thinking it over, then he reached out and took the large piece of goat cheese. Having accepted the bribe, the soldier turned and rode away without a word.

Hans and Jakob said nothing, but breathed a quiet sigh of relief. At least Amerika won't have soldiers who rob you on the road.

Ten

THE WINTER MONTHS PASSED slowly. The extreme cold of the last few years continued, but the killing frost had not come in September this year, and crops had not frozen before they could be gathered. Each family struggled to survive the winter and to quietly gather things to take along in Spring.

Wilhelm and Peter went back to Mosbach to help Captain Jager several more times. They loaded lumber from the mountain areas, cheeses from the farmers, and pottery made in the villages. They got to know the captain and trust him. On occasion they talked with him about their plans.

Captain Jager grew to like them, too. He often thought to himself, "They are better workers than most. They don't fight or steal like many workers I have hired on the docks along the river."

Once he sent a piece of wool saying, "Use this make coats for Daniel and Jorg." Captain Jager took a special liking to twelve year old Daniel who reminded him so much of the son he had lost not long ago.

❀   ❀   ❀

One evening the captain sat with his wife by the fireside in the house they had near Weinheim. "You know, Maria, I think I have just decided something. I don't know why it has taken me so long."

"Philip, when you get that look, it is going be something you have been thinking about for a while. What is it?" Maria knew him well.

"I have studied the figures and decided that if I offer those young men passage to Rotterdam for work, it will be a bargain for all of us. They can ride on my cargo ship and help as we go. The cargo will have more protection from thieves."

Maria stared at him with amazement. "You are talking in circles, Philip. Which young men? You hire dock workers all the time. You are always complaining about them! Now you want to take them to Rotterdam?" Maria had known this man all her life, and he always managed to amaze her.

"Maria! Maria! This is Daniel's family and their friends -- the boy who reminds me so much of our own young Johan Philip."

"Oh," said Maria. The memory of their own dear son was still a painful. "It will help you as much as them." Then she became thoughtful, "That means you will be gone longer than the usual couple of weeks. You don't always go all the way to Rotterdam."

"I think I need to expand my business a bit. There are many goods in Rotterdam that have come from England and other places in the world. There is a market for those goods here in Heidelberg and Mainz -- even in the cities farther south. And, more peasants are traveling to Rotterdam every day."

Maria wasn't fooled. "You are too soft hearted, Philip. You will get yourself into trouble helping these poor fools who think they will make it in Amerika!" She shrugged slightly, giving a helpless motion with her hands. "No use arguing with you when you have your mind made up!"

"Ah, Maria. You know me too well," Philip smiled and put his arm around her. "I need to do this."

Maria had a sixth sense that often amazed her husband, Philip. "I have a feeling these people are only a small stream in the river of emigrants that are about to come. If this Daniel is as bright as you think he is, you will find a way to keep him with you!"

Surprisingly, Maria's pronouncements were often correct. Philip was impressed. Why had he not thought of this? Maria was the daughter of a rich merchant and unlike many women of her day, she had an education. She associated with other women like herself and knew gossip the common public did not.

"Well, bring me something nice from Rotterdam and something for our niece's wedding next summer!" Maria smiled up at Philip. "I shall ready a room for an apprentice, just in case!"

"Ah, Maria," Philip sighed and gave her a kiss on the cheek. "How did I get so lucky to marry a woman as wonderful as you!"

She looked at him, her smile spreading over her lovely face and into her grey eyes. Devilishly she said, "Money!"

Eleven

As February was drawing to a close, three soldiers pounded loudly on the Meier's door, then walked in uninvited. They strode across the cooking room almost stepping on Inge who sat playing on the rug near the fireplace, their heavy boots tracking mud and snow across the floor.

The family had just finished dinner and were still sitting around the table. Wilhelm and Peter were in a quiet conversation about their day. They were stunned by the brazen entry. Katja stopped in the middle of clearing the dishes, staring at the bold visitors.

Standing in their uniforms, the soldiers looked menacing, as they demanded, "We are told by some of your neighbors that Jorg says you are going to run off to Amerika."

The family was momentarily silenced with fear, then, Grandfather laughed, "Ah, Jorg." He rose from his chair near Inge and moved toward the table where Jorg stood frozen. "He has such an imagination, this one! One day he is going to Amerika, the next day to Paris." He put his arm around Jorg's shoulders pulling the boy's fear into himself.

"Is that true?" the soldier pushed his gloved, finger into Jorg's chest, trying to scare him. His wolf-like eyes stared into Jorg's frightened blue ones. This particular soldier got a certain pleasure from scaring these dumb farmers.

Jorg couldn't utter a word. He simply nodded his head. He trembled with fright, but he was determined not to cry and to stand up quietly. He couldn't have spoken even if he wanted to.

The soldiers looked at Grandfather. They suspected the old man was hiding something. They walked around the room, their big riding boots making clomping noises on the stone floor. They were looking for signs that might lead them to believe the family was getting ready to run away in Spring without permission, without paying their fees, cheating the overlord who was in charge of the land. The soldiers knew if these peasants were going to run in Spring, they often had their belongings piled all over the house.

The family stayed near the table, speechless, riveted to their spots, afraid to say or do anything. These men had such power over them; they dared not irritate them.

The soldiers looked under the sleeping mats where they knew people usually hid their money. They carefully investigated every the corner of the two rooms. Katja held her breath that they may decide to look in the trunk; but

Peter had put it under the long table and made it look like it belonged there as part of the furniture. The cheeses and dried fruit were carefully hidden in the root cellar, the entrance of which was under the rug where little Inge sat wide-eyed.

"Frau Fenstermaker said Katja had two new dresses. Where did she get them? Why does she need *two* new dresses if she is not going anywhere?" the soldiers demanded.

Again, Grandfather saved the day. "That dress belonged to my sister's daughter-in-law. She is getting so fat she cannot get her big rear into it!"

The soldiers laughed because they knew this woman and knew she was very big. Her husband milked several cows, and it was said she loved the cream. People often made jokes of her size. They probably would not check the story.

The soldiers walked around the rooms again, then went outside banging the door behind them. They looked around the shed checking inside and out, turning everything upside down, but finding nothing remarkable. Finally, they mounted their horses and went on their way at a gallop.

As soon as the soldiers were well out of earshot, Katja landed on Jorg. "Jorg! You were told not to talk about this! For that we may just let you here with the neighbors! You can live in their barn by yourself and sleep with the chickens and cows and eat hay! What were you thinking?"

"I just told my friend, Josef Behm. I told him not to tell."

Jorg was shaking with fear, tears brimming in his eyes. "I told him because I will miss him very much. He is my best friend. I wanted to give him my favorite carved horse to remember me."

"Well tomorrow you tell Josef you changed your mind, and you are going to Paris to be an artist as soon as you are fifteen. If the soldiers check they will hear that part of the story. Do not say even one more word about Amerika or you *will* be living in the neighbor's barn with the cow!"

From her spot on the rug by fireplace Inge heard the word cow. She looked at Jorg with her cute little smile and said, "Muhe, Jorg," and they all burst out laughing breaking the terrible tension.

Twelve

WINTER BEGAN TO PROMISE Spring; the time for departure grew near.

IF THE NEIGHBORS ASKED questions they were told, "We are going to Heidelberg to visit Grandfather's relatives sometime this spring. His younger brother is not well. Grandfather asked his nephew, Adam, to take care of the goat, the pigs, the cow, the mule and the small farm while we are gone."

The day before they left, Katja said to Jorg, "Now you can tell your friend, Josef Behm, that we are going to Heidelberg to see Grandfather's relatives." Jorg was delighted to redeem himself and asked Josef to take care of his favorite wooden horse, Ritter, until he got back. Jorg gave Josef a special big hug. He explained, "It's for taking care of Ritter, Josef."

Each family would take one trunk. Wilhelm took all three

trunks with him at the end of February when he went to the dock with a load of wood for Overlord Frederich. They were put in the Captain's storage shed, later to be put on Captain Jager's boat as cargo.

Wilhelm, Peter, Hans, Ulrich and Jakob met the last day of February to review the final plan of the journey to Amerika.

Jakob and his brother, Hans, and Ulrich's family, would start on Jakob's boat which was small with just one square sail. It would be crowded, but it would work; being crowded would keep them warm in the chilly March air blowing down from the neighboring mountains.

Captain Jager had agreed that the four Meier brothers could come as his workers and no one would suspect them for they had seen them working previously on the dock. They would receive passage by working for him.

Captain Jager told Wilhelm, "Have Jakob and Hans stay near my boat with their scow. When they get a day or two downstream, they will not know the river. It can be treacherous at this time of year for the melting snow has made the water high and cold. There are rocks and swift water awaiting the inexperienced. When we get far enough away from Prince Elector's territory, they can sell the boat to a merchant in one of the river towns."

Since the captain could not have Katja and Inga on his river boat when it left Mosbach, they would be with Hans. That way Ulrich, Hans, and Jakob would look like young men with their families going to visit relatives in the north. That is what they told any who asked.

"When we get down the Neckar River, near the Rhine where we are not so well known, we will join the others on the boat," Jakob explained.

Grandfather worried that he was too old to make it to Amerika, but he said he wanted to go with the Captain as far as Rotterdam. "I'll just go along to Rotterdam and be the watchman on the boat dock. Then maybe, I'll return home." He really wanted to go along for the entire trip, but he thought he would be a burden and one more expense they couldn't afford. Still, there was a little voice inside him that whispered … maybe … maybe.

While lying awake on his sleeping mat, tears of sadness silently sliding down into his whiskers, Grandfather had thought about the journey . He tried to resign himself to the loss of all his wonderful grandchildren whom he would never see again. Most likely, in Amerika, the young ones would find someone to redeem the rest of their passage fees, but who would buy the services of an old man who had to walk with a stick?

❀   ❀   ❀

In the beginning of March, early on a Sunday morning, Adam, Grandfather's nephew, drove the family in the wagon to Mosbach. Adam guessed what was going on for it was strange that the two other families were going. However, Adam said nothing and asked no questions.

They were family and he wished them well. He knew he would be able to work the farm and live with Grandfather Meier. This would make him a very eligible husband for the pretty girl he wanted to ask to be his wife.

Captain Jager had furniture to load into his boat to be taken to Heidelberg where he would deliver it to the university. Ulrich, the carpenter, seemed to have good reason to be traveling with furniture. Wilhelm, Peter, Jorg, and Daniel began their jobs as sailors helping with the cargo.

At the dock, the others boarded Jakob's small scow as planned. The March wind was merciless. "Be careful when you step on the scow," Jakob cautioned. "The wind makes the water rough. It is unsteady. Step over the edge and into the middle of the boat. Don't fall in, the water is extremely cold."

Barbara and Katja huddled together for warmth, keeping the two young ones close. "I am so afraid they will fall in," Barbara worried. Jakob and Hans handled the scow because they knew the little craft well. Ulrich tried to keep everyone calm.

As they began their long journey, they all turned to look at the rising sun over their beloved mountains for the very last time.

Down The Rhine

Thirteen

YOUNG DANIEL WAS INTERESTED in learning how to keep track of materials on board. Captain Jager was happy to help him learn for he truly liked Daniel. "I will show you how I do that, Daniel. It is very important to be accurate." In spite of himself, the boy reminded him of his own bright son. Working with Daniel made Captain Jager happier than he had been since that loss. Daniel's 'young boy' enthusiasm made him take on his education with a pleasant mixture of energy and enthusiasm.

"By the time we reach Rotterdam, Daniel, you will be able to add and subtract and keep my cargo log. I will help you learn to read for that is important," Captain Jager told him as he showed him the log. He opened his account book to the numbers that kept track of the cargo information. "This part tells me what I have bought and sold."

It wasn't long until Daniel was learning how to count and write the numbers in the log. He was very proud of being the one in the family able to do this. Happily he showed his big brothers who smiled proudly at him, ruffled his hair with their big rough hands and said, "This is a wonderful thing to know, Daniel."

"Come here, Jorg, I want you to learn, too!" Daniel held out the papers to Jorg. Jorg watched everything that Daniel did and he, too, began to learn.

The captain called them his 'sea sponges'. They smiled, but they weren't sure what that meant.

Wilhelm and Peter thanked Captain Jager often for the interest he took in the two young boys for he was giving them an education they would have never gotten at home. "We know you are teaching things they will be able to use to make a better future. We are really appreciative for what you are doing and how you have treated us."

The brothers did extra things for the captain to show how much this meant to them for neither of them could read nor write. The Captain was giving Daniel and Jorg a chance they never dreamt they would have.

As they traveled down the Neckar on their way to the Rhine there was plenty to see. There were boats of all sizes on the river. People were working in the fields near the shore.

In a little more than a day, they could see the wall of Heidelberg. Captain Jager, pointed to the top of the Konigstuhl hillside said, "See the castle that looks down over the city."

Jorg's eyes followed the captain's finger. "It seems like some of it is falling down!" Jorg remarked squinting his eyes to make sure of what he was seeing.

"It is," Captain Jager said. "It was struck by lightning almost 200 years ago. Some of it was rebuilt, a little below the first one." He showed them again. "See the higher one? The Swedes attacked that one about a hundred years ago, and then the French nearly destroyed the town in 1693."

"No wonder it is falling down!" Jorg was thrilled to know all this. Stories of soldiers, knights, and battles excited him; he began to realize the world was much bigger than he ever imagined.

"The last time I was in Mannheim, I heard the Prince Elector is thinking of abandoning this castle at Heidelberg and moving his whole government to Mannheim," the captain added.

Captain Jager had to stop at Heidelberg to unload some of the furniture for Heidelberg University. He said they would start again early in the morning, so if they wanted to have something warm to eat, this would be a good place to buy a hot supper.

The four brothers went to work unloading the furniture into a wagon which had come to meet them. Grandfather kept an eye on things while they made the delivery. They were all very careful not be too generous in their answers to the friendly conversation of the Heidelbergers. They had not yet come too far from home.

Happily, the ones in the small scow took the captain's suggestion immediately. "I am tired of cheese and boiled eggs and we have only begun!" said Jakob to Hans as they tied the little boat to the dock.

They were all tired, stiff, and cold from sitting in the scow. They had been out only a day or so, and already they were feeling cramped and cold from the March air.

Along the Heidelberg dock area there were plenty of shops where they could buy soup or sausages. What a welcome relief from the cold meats they had brought with them, for this was the first time they went ashore since leaving Mosbach. It felt so good to stretch their legs and walk around. They all ordered warm soup and sausages from the Sausage House which they ate at one of the long tables set up nearby. "We'll take some of these sausages along for my brothers," Katja told Hans."Please order them for me."

Johannes and Inge ran and played, joyfully chattering their own childish language, celebrating the simple freedom to run and play in the sun.

Later as the three families sat on the deck at dusk Wilhelm asked, "We are on the way! How is it on the little scow?"

"Very cold and rough." answered Ulrich.

Nodding her head in agreement, Katja added, "Cramped and uncomfortable! And I am in constant fear that someone will fall into that ice cold water."

"Maybe we should talk to Captain Jager about selling the

scow at Mannheim. That would be just as we reach the Rhine."

"Yes," Ulrich said, "I think that is a good idea. I am willing to crowd into any space for some shelter from the wind for Johannes."

Barbara nodded in agreement, "It seems perfect to me." She would be relieved when everyone was a bit safer.

Captain Jager told them that as they got nearer the Rhine, they would have to stop every night in the safety of the dock waiting for daylight, because parts of the river were swift, full of rocks and dangerous spots. He needed to be able to see his way clearly in the daylight.

Fourteen

THE NEXT DAY DAWNED cloudy and windy with light March snow flurries as they left Heidelberg. Although it was a bit late in the year for the snow to pile high, the cold wetness of it chilled them through and through. The wind made the water rough causing the boat to bounce around.

The passengers in Jakob's little scow huddled close together to stay warm. Staying dry was not possible, for there was very little shelter on this small boat. It was not meant for passengers. The best they could do was spread a leather cover over them.

Inge and young Johannes suffered the most for they were toddlers shivering against the adults to stay warm. No one had much to say, for they were all concentrating on staying in the boat and huddling together for warmth. Although they wore their heaviest clothes, the March wind was relentless, the warmth and comfort of last night's soup and sausages were forgotten.

Ulrich put his hand on Jakob's shoulder, "I have a new

respect for how you and Hans handle this light boat in this swift water! I wish I could help you, but I see that the two of you are masters at it and know just what to do!"

Hans and Jakob kept the scow close to the captain's bigger boat. They stayed near to the shore as they did when on a trip for their shop. They had never had their boat this far away from home, and they didn't know the river here. They depended on Captain Jager to guide them.

They looked at each other, "I don't know if my arms have ever been so tired!" Hans groaned. Young as he was, the work was tiring because the trip was longer than any they would have taken for shop purposes.

"Every rock we pass is a rock closer to Amerika!" Jakob replied, trying to sound cheerful and keep the dream alive.

Barbara tied her scarf around Johannes' waist to make sure he didn't fall overboard.

Katja said, "That is a good idea, Barbara. It allows them to move a little, too." She did the same for Inge. Having no understanding or fear of the river, the two little ones were in constant danger of falling overboard into the deep, icy water. The worry of keeping them safe was beginning to show on the Barbara and Katja already.

They spent a chilly the night on board. This was terrifying because they could see very little in the darkness. It was good to know they were not far from Mannheim. They realized how difficult it would be to remain in this little boat all the way to Rotterdam as some fleeing peasants had done.

"I am certainly glad we will be transferring to the captain's boat very soon," Ulrich remarked. He tried to hug Johannes close to his body to share some of his own warmth.

❀   ❀   ❀

Jakob and Hans talked about the letter they left for Lucas. They were curious about whether he had found it. "I tucked the note in among my papers on the desk," Jakob said. "I instructed him to take care of his grandmother, Frau Gartner, and put some money aside for future needs." The less Lucas knew about exactly where they were, the better. They did say they would try to communicate after they had arrived at their destination and were settled.

"He will know," Hans said quietly. "I really think Old Frau Gartner knew. She just didn't let on."

❀   ❀   ❀

The early morning wind whipped around them and they shivered in the cold air, but by afternoon, the sun came out and warmed them. March was being unpredictable as only March can be.

They had been on the river all morning, when they passed a group of people in a small boat like their own floating down toward the Rhine. The folks in the other boat waved and smiled, but they looked exhausted as they huddled close together.

Ulrich noticed there were twelve people in that boat crowded so closely there was barely room for their knees. "That seems like too many for such a small craft no larger than this one!"

Hans studied the passengers in the other boat and said, "Jakob, I think you and I saw one of those men at the market in Eberbach. I think he was a taylor. I wonder if he is doing the same thing we are doing?"

"I think he is. I wonder if he knows anything about this river or the Rhine. We are really the lucky ones to have Captain Jager who knows the rivers, the rocks, and the current."

Inge whined and struggled to get out of Katja's lap, "I'm hungry, Katja."

"How about a boiled egg for you and Johannes?" Katja reached into the cloth bag and found one for them to share.

"No egg!" complained Johannes. He crossed his chubby little arms stubbornly, and put a determined look on his little-boy face.

"No choice, my dear," smiled Barbara. "It is good, try it." She pretended to eat it herself. That always convinced him.

❀   ❀   ❀

On the Captain's boat, Daniel and Jorg continued to learn how to count the stores on the boat. Captain Jager was enjoying teaching them how to write the numbers and understand what they meant. Daniel proved to be a smart young man with a mind that quickly mastered the information as the captain explained it. Like all teachers, the captain delighted in an able student.

Wilhelm and Peter were learning how to guide the bigger boat under the close supervision of the captain, for there were dangerous places even in the Neckar River. Its current changed as it began to flow into the Rhine. On this boat the sheltered area was small, since it was meant just for the captain and a few crew members.

"I like learning to steer this boat!" Wilhelm exclaimed. "Don't you think I am getting good, Little Brother?'

"Well, Big Brother, you are no river captain!" Peter joked. "You are better at guiding the mule!"

"I can see that the captain knows this river well. When I see Daniel and Jorg learning from the captain, I know this was the right choice for us even though it is difficult. They will have so much more in Amerika," Wilhelm said.

Peter nodded in agreement.

The four brothers and Grandfather had only brought bread and cheese on board with them, but they knew Katja and Inge were having the same. Grandfather had joked to Jorg earlier, "We will both be able to wear the same coat by the time we get to Rotterdam!"

Captain Jager, for his part, thought he had made a good bargain. He had good workers for the price of their labor and an occasional meal. He liked the four boys and could see that they were honest and hard working. Even though Grandfather didn't do much work, he was good company and the captain enjoyed trading stories with him.

Grandfather could always be depended upon to keep an eye on the boat when they were docked. Having Grandfather at the boarding gate was like having an old gander on the farm aggressively guarding the property! If anyone who looked suspicious came near the boat, he would point his cane and shake it at them yelling, "Get out of here, or I'll take this cane over you!"

The captain thought to himself, "If ever there was anyone who deserved a chance in Amerika, it is this family."

Fifteen

THE TRAVELERS WERE STOPPED for the night. Tomorrow they would start at dawn and be in Mannheim before noon; it was a very busy port located where the Neckar flows into the Rhine.

As the sun dropped behind the mountains, the moon began to rise shedding its peaceful silver light on the river. Suddenly, they heard yelling behind them near the shore. Hans, Jakob, and their passengers looked back. In the moonlight they could see the crowded boat they had passed earlier now close to the shoreline.

Ulrich said, "I think there is a person standing in the icy water close to the shore. Someone has fallen in!"

The wind carried the sounds clearly to the families in the scow. People in the other boat were pointing down into the river, "There he is! Grab him! Pull him into the boat!" The sounds of splashing and yelling carried across the water. Two of the men were trying to stabilize the boat by tying it to a tree stump along the shoreline.

Barbara cringed as she heard a woman's voice shriek, "Oh, my God! Help us!" It wasn't hard to imagine herself in these circumstances, for she had worried about her own son falling into the icy water.

The father's voice was clearly heard as he wailed, "My son! My son!" They could see him open his arms to receive the limp child from the person who pulled him from the river.

The mother, her sobbing voice carrying across the void, cried, "He is dead! My child! He is dead! God have mercy!"

"What will we do?"

"Build a fire. Try to warm him!"

Jakob, Hans, and Ulrich watched the younger boys who jumped onto the shore and began searching for something to use for a fire.

"Shall we help them?" Hans was ready to go.

"The child is gone. There is nothing we can do to bring him back. He was small and that water is as cold as ice. We have no way of helping them," Jakob replied sadly. He was right, even from this distance Hans and Ulrich could see the child was dead as he hung limply from his father's arms.

The young boys from the boat who had gone searching for firewood returned with a few handfuls of dried grass and some small sticks. As he watched them, Ulrich realized for the first time that he had seen no debris along the river. "People who live along the river gather all the fallen limbs for their own fire," he observed.

All the others from the boat were now going along the shore trying to find more fuel to add to the fire. Not much was available, but they did get a bit of warming flame going. It was obviously too late for the young child who had been pulled from the water.

Jakob said, "I have heard stories of people floating down the Rhine to Rotterdam and losing their lives in the process. I never thought I would see it."

Ulrich, Barbara, and Katja were sobered by the same thought. "What if it had been Inge or Johannes?" They hugged their little ones a bit closer frightened by the tragedy playing out across the moonlit water.

Sixteen

The next morning, the memory of last night's disaster and the grief of those parents lay heavily upon them. The episode left them sobered and worried. "What will they do now?" Barbara asked Ulrich. She couldn't forget the memory of that limp little boy lying in his father's arms.

"If they go back home, they return to the same things they were trying to escape," he told her. "And they will have this terrible memory." He put his arm around her. "They have to bury him along the shore and go on."

"How sad," Katja said quietly, still remembering the heartbreaking scene.

"We need to get out of this little boat," Hans said to Jakob. "That could have been one of us! It scares me when I think of it."

"Today we will stop at Ladenburg just before Mannheim. It may be a good place to sell. I will ask Captain Jager's advice and try to do it today."

"We are far enough away from home now. I think we could all go on the larger boat," Ulrich agreed.

They stopped at Ladenburg a short time later.

"Where are we?" Daniel asked the captain, looking at the half-timbered houses of the town located inside the city wall. "Is that another palace over there?"

"This town is Ladenburg. We are west of Heidelberg, Son," the captain said. "What you see is the bishop's palace, built almost six hundred years ago. It is very close to Mannheim." The captain loved telling Daniel about the places along the way. He loved Daniel's mind, always asking, always wanting to know.

"Then we must be in a different territory!" Jakob smiled as he heard the captain's explanation to Daniel. He clapped Hans on the shoulder. Good-bye Frederick! Goodbye Prince Elector!" Then, very unJakob-like, he made a sort of mocking bow as he spoke. It made Hans burst out laughing.

Hans turned to the captain, "Do you think we could sell the scow here?" He gestured toward the town.

"You may not get as high a price as in Mannheim, but I do think you may find a buyer here. Sometimes Mannheim merchants come here because they think they will get a better buy at this smaller port. You could take advantage of that."

He thought a moment, then added, "There are plenty

of Ladenburg people who travel regularly by boat to Mannheim. Let me check for you. I can ask without raising suspicion. I know many of the merchants here."

While Wilhelm and Peter were loading some fresh cheeses, pottery, and carved figures to be sold farther up the Rhine, Jakob and Hans went with Captain Jager in search of a buyer for their boat.

Captain Jager seemed to know everyone. When he entered the Ladenburg Biergarten, the other captains all waved to him and called loudly, "He! Philip! How is it going?" They clapped him on the back and inquired about his wife.

He asked around to see if anyone was looking for a boat and before long he had several interested people. "Come down to the dock," he said, "just after noon."

Before returning to the boat, the three men sat down to order a meal from the owner's wife. "The wife makes the best sauerbraten in the area!" the owner bragged. He was a huge man with a big smile, a big belly, big blue eyes and a shaggy light colored beard. He touched Jakob's arm and said, "Try it, boys!" He set a plate in front of each of them.

"He was right! This is the best I have ever eaten!" smiled Hans waving his utensils over the food. "Frau Gartner can't even equal this!"

"I am going to have a piece of the wife's apple pie, too," said Jakob, drooling over the site of it on the back counter.

They had enjoyed their meal so much, they began to feel just a bit guilty about their friends back on the boat eating cheese and bread. "Let's celebrate our achievement so far and take sauerbraten back for the others," Hans suggested.

Because he felt sure they would sell their little scow this afternoon, Jakob agreed. The owner's wife added a generous serving of fresh bread for them and sent them on their way with a container filled to the top.

By the time they got back to the dock, Wilhelm and Peter had finished loading the boat and they were all sitting along the shore enjoying the pleasant afternoon . When Daniel and Jorg spotted Jakob and Hans coming with a good smelling meal they were like two hounds on a trail. They were laughing and jumping around nearly knocking the crock to the ground. "Down! Boys!" Hans laughed, "It's like controlling a pack of hunting dogs!"

They were all so happy for the hot meal, they ate every bite and sat back to reflect on their progress so far.

"Captain Jager asked me if I would like to be a boat captain," Daniel announced much to the surprise of everyone. "I said I thought I might like that job."

Wilhelm and Peter read each other's thoughts as their eyes met. Katja asked, "Was he asking you just because he was curious or was he really asking you?"

"Just asking I guess," Daniel shrugged.

"What would you say if he did really ask you to be an apprentice?" Peter questioned. "That would mean you would stay here and not continue to Amerika."

"I know," Daniel replied with a thoughtful look on his face. "I know. I would be torn if I had to make such a choice. It would be like looking down two different paths, and wanting to explore both."

Seventeen

In anticipation of selling Jakob's scow, they moved the few belongings they had in the scow over to the other boat. It was a wonderful relief to be out of the wind, and it felt much safer to be all together.

Captain Jager helped Jakob and Hans make a good deal on the scow, and they were happy to turn her over to a new owner.

"Let me sew your money into the hems of your pants," Katja offered when they returned from making the sale. She looked in the trunk for her sewing materials. "Shall I just divide it evenly?" she joked mischievously.

"I'm the oldest!" Jakob smiled, puffing himself up a bit.

"I'm the smartest!" Hans gave him a brotherly shove. "And the cutest!"

Katja laughed at the two of them. "Well, you are the cutest," she agreed. "I'm not sure about the smartest. Jakob is really smart."

In the end Katja sewed it carefully in the hem of their extra pants and in the lining of Han's coat. She had divided her brothers money and, sewn it into their clothing just the same way.

❀ ❀ ❀

When they got to Mannheim, Daniel and Jorg were surprised to see it wasn't as big as they thought it would be. "Let's get the captain to explain it." Daniel suggested. "He knows everything!"

Always glad to be the captain who knows everything, he told them, "Remember the castle on the hill in Heidelberg? After the French left there, they destroyed Mannheim. Now it is being rebuilt, along with a new palace for the Prince Elector."

Jakob and Hans were following his conversation closely, too. As educated men, they wanted to learn as they went down the Rhine. Looking at the town, they noticed something peculiar. "See how the streets do not follow the curves and turns of the hills and the river the way the streets do in the other towns!"

"That is the Elector's idea," explained the captain. "Since he has to rebuild the town, he has designed the streets in squares! Sometimes the people around the area call this town Quadrastadt." He looked at the boys, "City of Squares."

"How very strange!" Hans marveled.

Jakob's business mind immediately grasped the sense of the idea. "It is easy to know where you are going! People can find their way to the stores and markets!"

Ulrich who was standing nearby said, "This is a good idea. This town is where the Neckar River flows into the Rhine. Perfect for business!"

"It is," said the captain. "However, because the two rivers come together here, the water is treacherous. We will dock and depart very early in the morning."

Just before sunset, they sat on the deck discussing the exciting new things they had learned. None of them noticed Grandfather had been missing since the meal, for he often retired early, saying he was very tired. Lately he seemed to tire easily, so they didn't worry when he had gone to rest.

It was Jorg who decided to find Grandfather and tell him all that he learned, but he had to search the boat for him.

"Grandfather, Grandfather, where are you?" Jorg finally found him sitting on the floor in the sheltered part of the boat near the cargo. "Grandfather, I came to tell you all I learned," Jorg was chatting excitedly, but Grandfather didn't even open his eyes. "Grandfather, are you alright? Are you sick?"

"I think I am just very tired. I have a pain in my arm. I'll be fine," Grandfather tried to smile and not worry his little pal. "Tell me all about what you learned, mein kleiner Kumpel."

Reassured, Jorg sat down leaning gently against Grandpa and chatted on telling all he learned about palaces and squares and rivers. He felt Grandpa's body against his, but he didn't realize Grandpa had slumped down even more than before.

Eighteen

WHEN THEY LEFT MANNHEIM at dawn they realized they hadn't seen Grandfather this morning. He was usually the first one on deck. Jorg remarked about sitting with him last night, and there Katja found him on the floor leaning against the wall, just as Jorg had said. He was very ill and seemed close to death; he was pale and he had not strength enough to lift his head.

"Grandfather, Grandfather," she shook him gently, but he barely opened his eyes. "Wake up, I have a hot drink." He seemed very weak and had trouble breathing. He mumbled something about his chest feeling heavy.

Katja was alarmed at his weak, unresponsive appearance. "Wilhelm! Peter!" Katja called as she ran to the deck to find her brothers.

By the time they reached the cargo area, Grandfather could barely speak. He lifted his eyes to them and whispered, "At least I got to Mannheim. You must make it all the way to Amerika for me." Then he closed his eyes and was gone.

Jorg hugged the lifeless body of his beloved Grandfather and cried, "No! No! You can't go! I need you!" Tears ran down his cheeks as he tried to hug life back into him.

It was too late. Only Grandfather's spirit would accompany them to Amerika.

The next small church they came to near the river was in Gernsheim. Jakob and Hans bought a small piece of sailcloth to wrap the body. They buried him, without permission, in the corner by the wall that surrounded the small churchyard. Ulrich tied together a wooden cross as a marker. There would be no stone to tell of the wonderful grandfather who rested here.

Even the Captain was saddened by his passing for Grandfather was the one whose spirit never flagged; the one who could rescue every situation with quick wit and words of wisdom. Like an old gander on a farm, Grandfather had chased away potential thieves with his cane and sweet talked officials who came asking questions.

The family remembered Grandfather's words saving them from the soldiers last year when they came to search the house. They remembered Grandfather's strength when their parents died. He had been the solid rock upon which they had all leaned.

Katja sewed the money from Grandfather's coat hem, inside the seams at the waist of Jorg's pants.

She also gave Jorg the small, smooth, white stone that

Grandfather had always kept in his purse - the one he called his touchstone. He had often told the family how he found it in a brook when he was a boy. He loved its smooth shape, its almost white coloring, and cool feeling.

She handed Jorg the smooth stone saying, "Put this in the purse Grandfather made for you. That way you will remember his spirit is near you."

Jorg touched it and smiled. There was Grandfather's love and courage right at his fingertips. Wrapping his fingers around it, Jorg held it tightly in his small hand, kissed it, and put it in the purse under his shirt. It would stay over his heart forever.

Because Jakob and Hans were the ones who could read and write well, they offered to send a message to Lukas when they got to Rotterdam. He could give the news of Grandfather's death to his sister and her family.

They left Gernsheim later that morning, for they could not tarry at that spot for too long. The town was small and they didn't want to answer too many questions or have the soldiers of this district called to investigate.

Nineteen

By the end of the day they would be near Mainz and Wiesbaden where Captain Jager planned to meet with other captains. They often met and traded information about the river conditions, both physical and political.

"I will have dinner with friends at the tavern and discuss business with the other captains," he said to Katja. "There are hot springs in Wiesbaden. The ladies and children can go to the hot mineral waters. I think there is a place to wash clothes." He thought this would relax them a bit after the recent ordeal. He paused for a moment, then added, "Wilhelm, if you and Peter stay with the ship, the other three men can take the boys to the men's area of the hot springs."

"You will see there are several parts to the springs. The wealthy people go the baths in the buildings, but the town's people go a little farther into a clearing in the woods area where the springs are more natural and free. It is just outside the city wall. There is a section for men and one for women."

"We need to do that!" Barbara smiled at the thought of bathing for the first time in three weeks. "I would feel safer if the men go too." She smiled at them. "I would be afraid to go alone."

The captain advised Katja and Barbara, "Take Grandfather's clothes and wash them, too. You will need them later. Grandfather was always on guard duty for the boat, and I felt it was in safe hands! I miss him, too."

Katja and the family were touched by the Captain's kindness and thanked him several times. Peter and Wilhelm told him how much they appreciated his thoughtfulness, "We know Grandfather is smiling, too," Peter told him.

Captain Jager took Ulrich aside, putting his arm around his shoulder he said quietly, "When we dock, I will find a person to take you to the baths and bring you back. Leave all your valuables here on the boat. Only take the money you need, several pfennigs. Don't discuss your trip with people you do not know."

Ulrich noticed the seriousness in the captain's face; he nodded and headed off to tell the others.

The group was ready to go as soon as they docked. A man the captain knew took them in his wagon to the hot springs just outside of the small town. They were chatting excitedly and didn't notice the tall, dirty, old woman wearing a worn coat and holding a cane. She was by the town fountain watching them closely as they departed for the baths.

Hundreds of years ago the Romans had discovered these springs and created the first baths. Parts were still used by the common people - women and children in one area, men upstream nearby.

As the two groups separated, Katja whispered something into Hans' ear. He nodded and turned toward their area.

Barbara and Katja removed their clothing down to their underwear, took Inge and stepped into the warm water. "It feels wonderful!" Barbara breathed a sigh. "Don't we wish we had this when we were back on Jakob's boat in the wind and rain!" She leaned back in the water, and relaxed. "It has been a difficult several weeks. I still worry that this trip is not a good idea. I have a bad feeling about it, but Ulrich sees it as an opportunity."

"I think we have about a week to go," sighed Katja. "I, too, feel like it has been a long trip and we have hardly begun! You are probably tired; we all are."

The girls washed Grandfather's clothes, the boys homespun shirts, and their apparel. After spreading them out to dry, they settled themselves by Inge who was having fun splashing in the warm, shallow water with a little girl nearby. Their squeals of delight drew smiles from the other women near the spring. Barbara and Katja relaxed for the first time in many days and shared their thoughts about the trip and their girlhood experiences. Soon they were laughing, allowing themselves to unwind a bit.

After enjoying the water, they put on their clean clothing and began to gather the things close to them.

Suddenly one of the other women yelled to them, and pointed toward the clothes they had spread out to dry. The girls turned and were surprised to see the tall, dark figure of an old woman in a long coat. She leaned on her cane as she bent over their clothes. When she noticed they had seen her, she grabbed an armful of the items nearest to her and ran. Katja yelled and ran after her.

Katja was a strong, young farm girl and she quickly shortened the distance between them. The old woman dropped most of her stolen goods and her cane, as she continued toward the woods still clutching Grandfather's old coat to her chest. Her victims weren't usually so determined or so fast!

"What did she take?" cried Barbara. She was immediately frightened for they could ill afford to lose anything, especially the money hidden in the seams and hems.

"I think she had a lot of clothing, but when we spotted her, she dropped most of it."

"She looked like an old woman, but I think that thief was much younger than she looked! She ran like a young man! We were certainly helped by the yelling of the other women. They must know the thief!"

In spite of herself, Barbara couldn't help laughing at the

memory of Katja sprinting away, "You ran like you were chasing the pigs into the barn!"

Katja sorted through their things, "Grandfather's coat is gone. We will probably miss that when we are onboard ship, but it is a small loss."

Barbara went to retrieve Inge who was still playing by the water. She returned, soaking wet Inge in tow, to go over the remaining clothing with Katja.

Barbara leaned her head near Katja's and asked in a low voice that others would not hear, "Was Grandfather's money sewn into his coat?"

"This very morning I took it out and sewed it into Jorg's pants!"

"Thank Heaven! She probably watches for people who are strangers, who aren't paying enough attention! She knows about sewing money in the hems, I'll bet! I hope the thief didn't go over where the fellows are. "

"Probably not. She knows the women bring the clothes here. Maybe she comes here all the time to steal things!" She remembered Wilhelm telling them about Father Josef's warning against thieves everywhere. "Maybe we have lost Grandfather's coat, but he is still with us and has taught us a valuable lesson!"

Fifteen minutes later they all met at the wagon. When Barbara told Ulrich what had happened, he said, "We saw that old woman but she didn't come near us. She thought you were easier prey."

Hans came over to Katja, jokingly he said, "I heard you were the heroine of the day the way you chased that thief!" He looked down into her blue eyes and thought that although he had known her all his life, he had never noticed what a wonderful person she was.

She laughed and replied, "I don't think he expected to be chased by a tough farm girl!"

Twenty

When Captain returned, they started downstream, planning on making a little more distance before darkness fell. When they docked for the night they had a good supper of fresh bread with butter and some bacon and beans all of which they had purchased at the Wiesbaden town market.

As they ate, Hans said in a quiet voice, "We asked Daniel today at the bath, what he was thinking about Captain Jager's suggestion that he become an apprentice on board ship."

"Thanks for talking it over with him Hans," Katja answered quietly. She could hardly bear to think of not having her little brother with them.

All eyes looked at Daniel who sat quietly, like he was deep in thought.

"It was good of you to bring it up, Hans," Peter replied. "I think he was worried Wilhelm and I would say no. Is that true, Daniel?"

At last Daniel lifted his eyes to his brothers and sisters. "I do think I would like to learn how to be the captain of a ship. I guess I am torn about leaving the family. Would you be angry with me if I did stay here with Captain Jager? Do you think Grandfather would have been upset?"

Jakob, always the one to see the logic, said almost as though he were thinking out loud, "It is an unexpected opportunity for you, Daniel. You are learning to read and write and understand numbers. You could become a ship captain some day and perhaps sail to Amerika with your own ship! You are just the right age to become an apprentice." He took Daniel gently by both shoulders, looked into his face, and said, "Take advantage of opportunity when it presents itself!"

"Not many get such a chance! And, Jakob is right, it is a perfect match for you," Hans agreed. "This could be a better chance than Amerika could offer as a redemptioner!"

"Oh, how we will miss you!" Katja said as she put an arm around him in a big hug. "But time will pass and you may still be in Amerika with us!"

"Yes, we will miss him, Katja, but we must support his choice when he makes it. It is the chance of a lifetime," Peter said.

Wilhelm, who had been listening to all this, agreed, "The

captain is a good man, better than most. He will be fair and honest with Daniel. Daniel will be like his own son. We don't know what our future holds, but he will know his future. I feel like good things will happen for him."

"You don't think Captain will try to turn him into the son he lost, do you? That wouldn't be so good!" Hans asked.

"I discussed that with him one day," Wilhelm confided. "I don't think he will do that. He is honestly looking for an apprentice, and he thinks he has found one. Do you feel that way, Daniel?"

"Yes, I really like him, and I love all that I am learning!" Daniel smiled. "I never thought I would be able to learn to read and write! Every day I learn so much from him about the river, the towns, the history!"

※ ※ ※

Just before they retired to the sleeping area, the captain brought them together to discuss the next day. "Tomorrow," he said, "we will begin to pass some of the ruler tyrants of the Rhine. They will have a chain extended across the river and they charge a toll to pass. They don't always come aboard, but they may. Put things out of sight tonight. Hide everything of value."

"What shall we do if they do come aboard?" Wilhelm asked.

"Throw them off!" Peter suggested in a loud voice.

"Oh no!" the captain said sternly, "Say nothing. Do nothing, unless you must protect yourself. It will only make things worse. If they think you are being difficult, they will be even nastier to you. They have all the power. They all know each other."

"I've noticed a good many small boats like Jakob's floating down the river. What will happen to them?"

"They will probably lose most of the money and possessions they brought with them by the time they get to Rotterdam," answered the captain. "When they can't pay the toll, the soldiers will take their things or worse. They may even take them as prisoners. I have actually seen a few of them killed!"

"That is terrible."

"Boys," Peter looked right at Daniel and Jorg, putting a hand on each boy's shoulder, "if they come aboard, do not speak to them! Do you understand?"

They both nodded looking very serious.

"Are there many of these places with chains?" Jorg was remembering the soldiers at their home that day which seemed so long ago.

"I'd say there about thirty castles between here and the border. They all do it. They usually demand money as a fee, but the other captains told me today that sometimes they will take goods as a bribe. I have been here before. I am ready for them. The important thing is to protect our cargo by not making them think they must search the boat."

This was very sobering.

Ulrich noticed Barbara's face. She was obviously afraid for herself and for Johannes. Not for the first time, Ulrich began to rethink the wisdom of his decision to go to Amerika with his small family, but for the moment, he said nothing. He just lifted Johannes up on his arm and put the other one around his trembling wife.

Twenty-One

BEFORE THEY GOT TO Bingen they passed a few islands in the middle of the river from which several large iron chains stretched across to the shore. Guards stood in the tower built on the island, where they had an excellent view of river traffic.

"Halt!" they yelled, their voices carrying across the water loud and clear as their comrades cranked up the chain, impeding the way. Immediately several soldiers started out toward the boats caught in the chain.

These men were not much different from the soldiers that had come to search the Meier household -- gruff, demanding, making an effort to be as terrifying as possible.

The two boys, Daniel and Jorg, peaked out at the tower and the soldiers from their hiding place in the cargo area. They saw castles on both sides of the Rhine.

"I think they are sometimes from a castle on the east side

of the river, sometimes from the west side," whispered Daniel. "Their uniforms are only a bit different. "

"They are probably the uniforms of their prince," Jorg whispered back. He noticed their bright colored coats, tall hats and high boots. He trembled as he noticed some had a large sword hanging from a belt; others had a bayonet fixed to the end of a musket.

Daniel carefully studied the behavior of the soldiers, "See how they threaten the people in the small boats by poking them with their bayonets so they pay the fees." His heart was pounding as he watched them even though he knew he and Jorg could not be seen.

There were two small boats nearby like the one Jakob and Hans had. The soldiers were especially demanding of those people, making them get out of the boat. The boys could hear the soldier's demands as their voices carried across the water: "Where are you going? Where are you coming from? Why are you on the river?"

The voices of the people were full of fear as they tried to answer without irritating the soldiers. Soldiers always came to the travelers in small groups of two or three and stood close with their weapons clearly visible. Seeing them pushing the people or searching them made the boys tremble. Grabbing one man they threw him into the water. This man was a lucky one for he knew how to swim even though being thrown into the cold water with all his clothes on made it difficult.

Daniel and Jorg felt lucky to be with Captain Jager because each day they drew closer to the mouth of the Rhine, they saw more small boats manned by fleeing groups, subjected to the aggressive armed guards. The soldiers knew these people were trying to get to Rotterdam to escape, and they enjoyed taking their possessions and terrorizing them.

"They scare me," Jorg said, his voice trembling with anxiety. His hand reached into the little purse and touched Grandfather's stone. He felt Grandfather's calm spirit immediately and relaxed slightly.

Finally the soldiers brought their small boat over to the captain's vessel and came aboard. Immediately they demanded a fee which the captain paid without argument. They looked over the adults on the deck, but made no move toward them. They let him go on without searching the boat because they had seen him before on the river. After asking a few questions, they left.

By the time the captain's boat got to the small town of Assmannshausen they had passed a number of such places, paid the fees, and survived the forces of various princes. Here at Assmanshausen they docked for the night. The surrounding hillsides were covered by vineyards famous for their red wines which they sold to the boats along the river.

Captain Jager motioned Wilhelm, Peter and Daniel to come with him. "I am going to buy some wine to sell later for it is considered to be among the very best. I plan to get some to barter with the soldiers. You come along to do the loading."

When they were on the hired wagon heading to a nearby vineyard, the Captain said, "I will soon need to know what you have decided, Daniel. You are a bright boy, and I really think you could do well as a ship captain. There will be much to learn but in ten years or so you could actually be in charge of a ship! In ten years you will be a young man, not much older than your brothers are now."

"I am thinking I am going to do it," Daniel responded. "I am torn about leaving my family, though." He had struggled with this since it was first mentioned.

"We talked together at Wiesbaden," Wilhelm responded. "He is considering this seriously. We don't want to see him separated from the family, but we do agree you have been very generous in your offer. He is just the right age, too."

"Jakob thinks that your offer has less risk than what we are doing, since we have no money and will have to be redeemed on Amerika's shore," Peter remarked. "There is a good chance that we would be split up. That could be worse, since Daniel is young and would have to serve until he is an adult."

"It will take Peter and I at least five years of work in Amerika to pay for our ship passage. By that time, Daniel will have learned to read and write and be almost ready to take charge of a ship!" Wilhelm added.

"You know, this was the plan I had for my own son who was taken from me by smallpox last year," the Captain confided. " I know Daniel is not my boy, but I will take care of him and teach him well." He looked at the serious faces before him and placing his hand on Daniel's shoulder, he added, "You will not be sorry. You will be treated well."

❀   ❀   ❀

While they waited on the boat, Hans suggested to Jakob, "Let's go to the market place and get some wine for supper. Ulrich can be in charge for an hour."

"Great idea, Brother!" and off they went, returning soon with a treat for all.

"This is a pretty little town." Hans nodded toward the hillside and told the others, "See that old church in the distance, we were tempted to visit it but decided that would not be a wise choice right now."

Jakob added, "Because of the statues I thought it may be a Catholic Church."

"We did visit the butcher, though!" Hans pulled out a few sausages from the cloth bag over his shoulder and two fresh loaves of bread. He smiled the charming smile that had won him many friends and customers in the past. However, this smile was for Katja alone.

Jakob watched Hans divide the sausages while Katja sliced the bread. His mind wandered back to comments Hans had made to him recently. He had remarked that although he had known Katja all his life, he never noticed how pretty she was and vulnerable, until the death of Grandfather and the incident with the thief at Wiesbaden. Jakob smiled. Maybe this journey will bring a development they hadn't considered.

Rotterdam

Twenty-Two

THE GROUP SURVIVED A few more days of slow progress, frightening chains, soldiers, and fees. Soldiers frequently inspected everything and once took things from the passenger's trunks, things they could hardly spare. When that happened, the families struggled to stay quiet, feeling afraid and angered at once, but they reminded themselves they were nearing Rotterdam.

They all breathed a sigh of relief as the mountains of Europe began to give way to the flat lands of the Netherlands. The waters of the river became rougher near the deltas where several rivers flowed into one, and finally into the North Sea.

Wilhelm, Peter, and Katja stood on the deck, and looked out at their disappearing homeland. "I feel a strange mixture of sadness and happiness," remarked Peter. He put his arm around Katja whom he could see was very emotional at the moment.

"I feel just a bit of fear," added Katja. "It is not only the life we will never see again, but also the unknown experiences that await us in a new land."

"I never dreamed we would be doing this. It fills me with all those feelings, plus an excitement for the future I hope we will find," Wilhelm said. They stood together, arms around each other, with the never ending wind of the Netherlands blowing on their faces.

Ulrich, who had paid much attention to the construction of the captain's ship and others along the river was now intrigued by the different vessels they began to see. Often he questioned Captain Jager about their designs.

"I never saw ships this size," he said, pointing to one nearby with tall masts and large, square sails. "These are clearly made for the waters of the ocean, not river sailing!"

"The Netherlands and England are known for shipbuilding, Ulrich," the captain told him. "Several other rivers flow into the Rhine here and it forms a delta at its mouth; Rotterdam sits on the North Sea. You'll see bigger vessels with more sails. The wind is strong here and colder."

Ulrich thought to himself, "I have spent my life building things. If Barbara and I decide we cannot to go on to Amerika, I could build ships, I'm sure." He knew Barbara was growing less and less fond of the idea of crossing the ocean. The river had been quite enough for her, and Johannes was not doing well either. Ulrich was worried for both of them.

Daniel came over by Ulrich and the Captain who was pointing out a few of the various ships. "The big ones with the high bow are the old galleons. That is a sturdy ship, but slow, created by the Spanish and modified by everyone else!" He laughed at his own joke and continued, indicating still another vessel, "The Dutch have created the Fluyt. That is this one to the starboard side."

Daniel's eyes followed and he noticed, "I see that is lower and sits in the water better. It seems like it would be better in a storm."

"You are right, my boy. You are going to be a good seaman!" the captain, smiled at him and patted him on the shoulder. "They are eighty feet long and usually are made for cargo. They are faster than the old galleons. Now, they have begun to take a few passengers."

Jorg came out on the deck, too, to view the city now easily seen across the water. He got very excited at all the different ships. "All these ships have different kinds of sails! Some are large and square, some are small and more pointed," he called to Jakob and Hans as he indicated the ones nearer the shore.

They observed the wharf of Rotterdam from the deck as they drew closer and closer. Jakob said, "This looks like a thriving business area. There are wagons of cargo on the docks loading and unloading!"

"It is certainly a busy place! It worries me a bit though, Jakob, look at the crowds of people who seem to be travelers like us," Hans observed. Whereas, Jakob saw business, Hans always saw people.

They could feel their smaller vessel being tossed more and more by the rougher water. It was then that Barbara came to join them, holding Johannes in her arms. She gave a worried look at Ulrich and said," I am becoming more worried about our son. He is listless, and warm to the touch. He doesn't want to play or eat. Even Inge couldn't get him to chase the birds off the deck with her. He just sat and held his head as she tried to get him to play."

Ulrich took the boy into his own arms and noticed how hot he felt to the touch. Once again, he began to worry about what would happen if Johannes was sick and they wouldn't allow them off the ship.

Soon the boat pulled up beside the dock and they were ready to join those crowds of people looking for shelter and lodging. Wilhelm, and Peter helped the captain unload his cargo of wine, furniture, lumber, and products from the Rhine farmland.

Then the family gathered round Daniel to wish him well on his new apprenticeship. It was difficult to say good-bye, but they tried to think about the great opportunity for him.

"I am really going to miss you, Daniel," Jorg said. He hugged him tightly as he could. "I don't remember a time when we have been anywhere without each other! But I promise, I will learn to write and I will write to you so you can find us in Amerika."

Daniel held on to Jorg and whispered, "I love you little brother. Don't worry. We will be together again, I just know it!"

Inge, who didn't quite understand the arrangement asked as she danced around her brother, "Are you going to sail us to Amerika, Daniel, on one of those big ships we saw?" The breeze was playing with her golden curls as she pointed to the biggest ship at the dock.

Daniel hugged her and thought to himself, I must remember exactly what she looks like so I can recognize her someday in Amerika.

As they were saying their last goodbyes, an inspector, dressed in a blue and white uniform with buttons carved from sea shells, came on board to question the families who were traveling on. There were so many Germans starting to come down the Rhine lately, he was getting impatient with them. He stood before the them, scowling, his white whiskers making him look like a growling dog. "Who is first here? Tell me where you are going, how you are paying."

Jakob and Hans, who were less afraid of him than the others, stepped up and told the inspector, "We have cash for two passages, plus one trunk. We want passage to Philadelphia."

The inspector directed them to the place just off the wharf where they could secure passage. He added, "It will be four guilders each." Then he grumbled to himself, "at least two of them have money, that's new! To them he said, "You can ask at that inn on the corner for a room for the two of you."

Then he turned his attention to Ulrich, "Is something wrong with the boy?" He looked closely at Johannes. "We don't want sickness brought into Rotterdam. If he is sick he can't leave the boat."

That comment and way the inspector looked when he ask, struck fear into Barbara, "I think it is just the rough water, he was fine when we were on the river." She tried to sound like it was nothing although she knew that wasn't quite true. She worried that it was more than that.

Ulrich, wanting to turn the inspector's attention away from Johannes, stepped up to him and said, "We need two passages to Philadelphia. What are the rules for a small child like Johannes?"

"Four guilders or four pounds for each adult, half for a child five years to ten years. How old is this child?" The inspector eyed Johannes again, trying to decide if the mother was telling him the truth about his not being ill.

"Then I guess we should go with Jakob and Hans," said Ulrich and took Barbara's arm, steering her toward the area where Jakob and Hans stood waiting to be released from the boat.

"Wait a minute, young man!" cried the inspector loudly. "What are you taking with you? Are you paying cash?"

"Yes," Ulrich answered," we have the eight guilders, and we have only one trunk. The boy is not yet three years."

"Move on then!" he turned his attention to next group of dirty looking travelers.

The inspector asked Wilhelm, "Are you all in one group? How old are these children?"

In spite of the fact that the inspector held great power over him at this moment, Wilhelm stayed calm and said, "We have four guilders for my sister, Katja. The little girl is three years. She will probably turn four by the time we reach Amerika."

"Well, what about the rest of you?" growled the inspector, wrinkling his brow and waving his hand toward Jorg who stayed close to Peter and Katja. "Here come the penniless ones," he muttered to himself.

"Wilhelm answered, "The boy is just nine, so he will go at half price, with Katja." He pulled from his purse the two guilders that Grandfather had saved. Even though that was nearly the last of their money, he and Peter had decided to use it for Jorg since Daniel was going to take the apprenticeship. That would save Jorg from being a redemptioner until he was an adult.

Wilhelm looked directly at the inspector and finished,

"That is all the money we have, so my brother, Peter, and I will have to be redeemed at the port of Philadelphia."

"Go with the others. Be sure to tell them you have <u>no money</u>," the inspector emphasized 'no money'. "You will have to sign a paper with the captain of the boat that gives you passage."

They all got off Captain Jager's boat with their trunks in tow and headed toward the office where the passages were sold. They looked back to see Daniel waving from the deck as the new men the captain hired began to load goods on board.

From here they could see the strong, tall man he would become, but they were too far away to see the tear in his eye.

Twenty-Three

THEY WALKED TOGETHER PAST the small tavern, the cheese market, and the fountain, then turned the corner where they saw a sign which Jakob read aloud as **PASSAGES, JENSON HOOGH.**

Jakob stepped up and spoke in German to the man in charge who seemed to understand very well, "We are all trying to get passage to Philadelphia on the next ship."

Jenson Hoogh replied in German, "The *Good Queen* out of Great Britain, under Master Thomas Martin, is sailing in about eight days. The next one, *William and Sarah*, is another week after that. The *Good Queen* has room for 100 passengers in an area built above the cargo hold. She is not yet full."

Jakob turned back to the others with a questioning look.

"Eight days will eat up a lot of money, but we have no choice," Peter answered for all of them. "Let's do it. Maybe we can find some work to make a few shillings."

Pushing a paper across his desk, the passage clerk said to them, "The men have to sign the ships list: first name and last, destination, and where you are from. Write how many are in your group. If all of you are going this will give Captain Martin almost a full ship."

Jensen Hoogh was a little friendlier than the inspector at the dock. He wore a loose white shirt much like the Germans wore but there were two things none of them had ever seen before -- wooden shoes, and round glass objects on his face that fit in front of his eyes.

Inge's eyes were glued to those wooden shoes, but Katja gave her that 'don't-say-a-word look' and with great difficulty, she managed to keep still.

After Jakob and Hans paid him and filled out the paper, he moved on to Ulrich who also paid the money for the two of them and signed his name on the list.

Then Herr Hoogh peered through his spectacles at the Meier family. "We are paying for my sister Katja and the oldest child, that should be one and a half passages," Wilhelm told him. "The two of us," he touched his brother's arm, "must be redeemed in Philadelphia."

Jensen frowned at him, "What about the girl?" He pointed to Inge who was slowly inching ever closer to those fascinating wooden shoes, trying to touch them with the toe of her own.

"We understand she is no charge because she is not yet

four years." Wilhelm tried once again to keep his voice pleasant and calm.

Herr Hoogh pushed the paper toward Katja, "Sign this, traveling alone with two children."

Quickly Hans came to her aid saying, "I will write their names for them; they can make their mark."

Herr Hoogh turned his attention to Wilhelm and Peter, "Now you two, sign as two brothers," Again, Hans came to their aid and wrote names for both of them. They made their mark beside each name.

"You must sign this paper, too, saying your fees will have to be paid by the person or persons who redeem you. If no one redeems you, you will be sold to someone on the dock for the price of your fees. Do you understand this?"

Wilhelm and Peter nodded. Hans wrote for them, and again they made the mark which would assure their fate on the other side of the ocean.

"You do realize," Herr Hoogh continued, "one person may not want to redeem both of you. You may go different places."

Wilhelm and Peter nodded. They would deal with that when they got to it. Now, they just wanted to get on that ship.

They all turned and filed silently out the door. Out on the sidewalk, the silence turned to noisy cheers of success!

They all broke into cries of joy, laughing and hugging each other to celebrate this milestone on their journey.

"Jakob and I will get a room and later in the week you can come there and get a bath and clean clothes," Hans told them. "Meanwhile, you need to find the camp which they provide for passengers. I think a saw a sign pointing that way." He pointed down to the end of the same street. The two Kramer brothers turned and began to walk toward the inn.

As the others stood looking with indecision down the street, an older woman approached them and said in German, "The camp is just down this street. There is a group there called, British Charities." She smiled at them as she spoke. "They will show you where to go. It is crowded, many others are there, too." She pointed to a large barn-like brick building. It stood out among the smaller houses that lined the street.

Ulrich and Peter lead the way past the small houses. Each house had a flower box hanging at the bottom of every front window. When they left Mosbach it was early March, rainy, cold, and dreary. Now, it was early April and some of the first flowers in the boxes were starting to bloom. The sight lifted their hearts as they walked along.

Soon they came to the large white building crowded with immigrants like themselves. Its appearance made them think it may have once been a barn or a wagon shed, but now the inside was simply empty space with a huge fireplace on one side. They found a corner spot to sit down and in minutes a woman came over. She was dressed in a long black and white dress, like the one worn by the lady who had spoken to them on the street. She, too, smiled pleasantly, "Do you have passage on a ship?"

They explained what they had and she replied, "We are British Charities. We try to give you a place of shelter for a week, so you are not out on the street. You will find some soup over by the fireplace. You can get water at the well in the square where there is also a market place. The chamber buckets are outside behind the building."

This woman wore the same type of shoes Jenson Hoogh had worn. This time Inge could not resist, she reached down to touch them, "Do those shoes hurt your feet? Are they made of logs?" she asked the lady.

The woman laughed out loud, "Would you like to try them on?" She slipped out of them and pushed them over to the little girl.

Inge clomped around in a circle saying, "Look at me, Jorg. I'm a Dutch lady with wooden feet!" Finally, she had to give them back.

The lady smiled and said, "You look a lot like a little Dutch girl with your pretty blonde curls."

By this time, Johannes was beginning to cough. Barbara felt his head and turning to Ulrich said, "He is very warm now, Ulrich."

"They won't let us on the ship if he is sick. I will get him some soup, maybe he will eat a little." Ulrich went off to the fireplace area with a small cup in hand.

"Jorg and I will go get a small bucket of water," Katja said. "Maybe a cool cloth on his forehead will help him. Come Inge, go with us." She held out her hand to her little sister.

Wilhelm and Peter went back to the area near the dock to see if they could find some work. They found a man at the Waag House who would pay them two shillings for the week to help him load things on and off the scales. They took the job, even though it was hard, heavy, tiring work, the pay was good. They were not afraid of work. Every penny would count when their ship stopped in England.

Twenty-Four

THE CONDITIONS IN THE large open space of the shelter offered no privacy, and few comforts. The air was filled with the smell of unwashed bodies. Although the stay at Rotterdam was rather short -- for most about a week or so -- the situation made it difficult. They had been there not quite a week, now.

Barbara sat close to Katja, speaking in a low voice, "I never dreamed we would be in a place like this! It is not very clean; the soup and bread is good but meager. Over and over again I wonder if this was the right decision. What if we lose Johannes! I am so afraid!"

"Keep the end in mind, Barbara," Katja answered gently, trying to lift Barbara's spirits. "I have noticed the wind here in Rotterdam never seems to stop blowing! I am glad we are not out on the street. Besides, it is safe here, and I am glad for that. The young ones can run and play together safely."

"You are right, I must think that way, Katja," Barbara said, feeling a bit ashamed of herself. She stood up and stretched her arms and legs, trying to will herself to relax.

It was then that she noticed the two Mennonite ladies, dressed in dark colored clothing, approaching them as they walked to the soup kettle. Their plain clothing gave them a somber appearance, but in fact they turned out to be quite friendly. As they drew near they smiled at Johannes, sitting by himself on the blanket coughing. Barbara nodded a greeting.

Stopping to talk to Barbara, they asked, "What is the little boy's name? Is he ill?"

Again Barbara nodded.

"We are sisters. She is Clara and I am Elisabeth," the taller one told them indicating her sister who looked to be about the same age as Katja. "We've come from Basel, Switzerland. Are you going to Philadelphia on the *Good Queen*?"

"Ja," Katja smiled. "You have come even farther than we have!"

"Ah, a long trip it was," they said with a gesture of weariness. "There is a group of us, that makes it easier. We help each other."

Then Elisabeth said, "I believe we have some medicine in our trunk to help with his cough. Would you like to try some?"

They went back and brought it to Barbara. "It is tea. Just steep it in water and give him a little sip of it," they directed. Then, they continued on their way to the soup kettle.

Barbara gave Johannes the sip of medicine, hoping this would be the thing that helped him.

❀   ❀   ❀

As Barbara and Katja chatted about the people they had met so far, Hans walked in the door searching over the area for them. His eyes landed on Katja and he smiled as he hurried over. "I have good news! I talked the innkeeper into allowing you to get a bath in our room. He is heating the water now. Take the children and clean clothes for all."

Quickly they gathered up all that they needed and followed Hans.

As they arrived the last of the hot water was being poured into the large metal tub that sat in the middle of the bedroom floor. It was almost full to the top.

"Wash the children first, then I will take them downstairs while you take a bath. Wash all your clothes last," Hans instructed them. Handing them the innkeepers strong soap, he headed downstairs to wait.

Soon Katja brought Johannes, Inge, and Jorg down to Hans, then headed upstairs again to Barbara who was now basking in the still-warm water. "Oh this feels so relaxing," she said. "I won't take too long, though, or you will have cold water!"

"Did you have a tub like this back home?" Katja asked her.

"We did, but not nearly so large! A big one like this takes too many trips to the well!" laughed Barbara.

"And, it takes a long time and extra wood to heat all that cold well water! Ours was much smaller than this, too," Katja remarked. "It was really just a wooden washtub that Wilhelm made."

When it was her turn Katja leaned back, washing her hair in the water. "No one else in that shelter has this!" she declared with a satisfied smile.

Finally, they washed all the clothes, getting them ready to hang around their trunks back at the shelter.

Katja said, "If we find a place to put these wet clothes outside, they will be dry in a few minutes in this wind!"

When they got downstairs they found Hans playing with the children and showing them the windmills in the distance. Katja smiled up at him and said, "Hans, do you think you can do this for Ulrich, Wilhelm, and Peter?"

"I will try, Katja," he smiled down into her blue eyes and thought she looked so pretty, he would do anything she asked. He didn't tell her how much he had to bribe the innkeeper to let shelter people use his tub.

Twenty-Five

THE NEXT DAY, THEY got word to come to the *Good Queen*. They gathered all their things and headed down to the wharf with some of the others from the shelter.

The *Good Queen* looked large compared to Captain Jager's small river boat. This was a wooden ship with three tall masts, each equipped with large square sails. There were even several cannons on the main deck with wooden boxes of cannon balls placed nearby.

Strong looking sailors worked on deck, dressed in light colored pants of a durable-looking material. Some were barefooted, some had low, tight shoes good for climbing the ropes. They hurried to and fro readying the boat for departure, winding ropes, checking sails, bringing barrels of water from the town fountain. They did not look at nor speak to the passengers coming onboard.

One of the captain's mates showed them to the ship's passenger deck. It was just down three ladder-like steps below the main deck.

Ulrich walked down the steps and studied his surroundings with his carpenter's eye. "They simply added this passenger area over the cargo. It doesn't seem like it was built here originally." He could see it was just a plank floor, like an extra empty room.

He looked back at the other men, "It is going to be very cramped here and stuffy. There are no windows and very little light. Let's put our trunks near the side of the ship, then at least other people will only be on three sides of us."

Peter found a spot and put the Meier trunk down. Jakob and Hans were right behind, placing their trunk to form another side. When Ulrich placed the Holtzmann trunk, it formed a sort of low wall around a space about as long as a man would be tall if he reached his hands above his head. It was not much wider than three or four people would be when lying side by side.

Peter immediately saw the wisdom of Ulrich's advice, as others set up their trunks in the middle of the floor, jostling each other for space. Each group tried to find a spot where they could spend their long ride.

"This is not going to be a very comfortable spot for many weeks travel!" groaned Wilhelm as he settled down near Peter and Katja. He could feel his muscles cramping in protest already.

"At least we got here as soon as they called us. The late comers will be even more crowded!" Ulrich observed. "I can't imagine how they will get one hundred people in this space! I am the tallest one of our group. You can see I can barely stand up straight!"

As more families arrived, everyone had to squeeze over a bit more to make room for the last ten passengers; that meant they had even less space than they thought they were going to have. It was impossible to lie down without touching the people beside you.

They sat on the floor of the deck together listening to the sounds of the other voices as each group tried to find ways to be comfortable. The smell of many bodies began to fill the space, for most of them had not had the opportunity for a bath before boarding; they had been wearing the same clothes for weeks.

Katja waved to the Mennonite women they had met in the shelter. They were with their group on the other side of the passenger deck. She touched Barbara's arm and said, "Look the Mennonites have children with them. Our three will have someone to play with. That is good."

Finally, when all the passengers were on board, the captain's mate came with the list from Jensen Hoogh to check names, and destinations.

"There is certainly no privacy here," Barbara complained, her eyes traveling over the room, taking in the close quarters.

"We can put Johannes and Inge end to end with their feet

toward each other," suggested Katja. "That will give us a bit more space. If you and I lie on either side of the little ones, Jorg can sleep at our feet. We are shorter than the men. They can sleep on the outside of the group."

"Let's try it that way," Barbara agreed. Although she tried to sound cheerful, she was feeling more and more uncomfortable about this journey. Every new event increased her uneasiness. She couldn't imagine making it through this trip in a space smaller than the stall their milk cow, Gretel, had in the barn of her childhood home.

Peter looked over the situation and asked, "It appears that we will sleep on the floor without a pallet. How many blankets did we bring? Perhaps we should at least make sure they are on the top of the things in the trunk while it is still daylight and we can see!"

❀   ❀   ❀

The ship's Master called them all to the upper deck just before they were ready to depart Rotterdam. He stood before them dressed in his uniform of dark blue. He wore a dark-colored, oiled hat with a wide brim that hung down almost to his shoulders to protect him from the weather, sun and rain. The constant wind ruffled his collar.

Using one of the sailors as an interpreter for the non-English speaking passengers, he said in a loud voice, " I am the ship's Master, Thomas Martin. The *Good Queen* will cast off within the hour."

He didn't smile, but behaved and sounded much as the overseers these people remembered so well. "You will get a daily water ration per family which will be for washing, cooking and drinking. There will be two meals per day -- morning and evening. The crew will pass out a covered chamber bucket which you will use in your quarters and which will be emptied in the morning and at night."

As he spoke, he looked them over closely, his practiced eye assessing them as a living cargo, the way a farmer might look over a herd of goats. He continued in his commanding voice, "The crew is the crew of this ship. You will not talk to them or bother them as they work. They are employed by the Queen of England. They are not here to help you."

He paused to see that his rules were understood. "We will stop in England, probably Cowes or Portsmouth, to log in with authorities and get permission to go to Philadelphia. The *Good Queen* is a British ship."

He took no questions. He simply turned and walked away, leaving the crew to dispense the buckets and the water ration.

England

Twenty-Six

THE PASSENGERS COULD TELL by their lack of sea legs when the big square sails of the *Good Queen* unfurled and she began to move into the windy North Sea. As they headed southwest toward the English Channel, the waves rocked the boat making walking difficult, for most of the passengers had never been on anything more than a small boat on the river.

The fresh air of the main deck beckoned them to escape the increasing smells of the passenger area below. There they sat on the floor, trying to stay out of the way of the sailors who were moving back and forth, getting the ship underway.

"Oh, how do those sailors climb up the masts like that without falling?" Jorg asked Jakob and Hans as he sat with them watching the activities. "They must be strong to wind that big rope! I tried to pick it up a while ago and I couldn't even lift it!"

"They are strong men," agreed Jakob. "A sailor must show he is able to lift a lot of weight before he is hired."

"Where will we be stopping for the night?" Jorg asked for that is what Captain Jager always did and he had always looked forward to each stop and each new city.

"We won't need to stop until we get to England," Hans explained smiling at Jorg's curiosity. "We stopped on the river because Captain Jager had to be able to see the rocks, sand bars, or other things in the river. We don't need to do that here."

"You mean we don't stop at night or anywhere until England? And, after England, not until Amerika?" Jorg's blue eyes grew wide with amazement as he began to realize the size of the ocean.

"That's right," Hans laughed at Jorg's surprised expression. "We will probably have plenty of time to practice reading and writing, since we can't go anywhere."

"Well, that is good, because I really want to learn to read and write. I promised Daniel I would." Jorg was so excited about the prospect of reading and writing, that Hans gave him a little hug. It was good to have this little boy along who had enthusiasm for everything.

Inge and Johannes came to the deck with Ulrich to join Jorg. "It is windy up here!" Inge laughed, her curls blowing in the breeze as she danced around in circles with her arms

146

extended. She was enjoying the wind and the movement of the boat didn't seem to bother her at all.

"Johannes, look up at the sails! See how the wind blows them out? It makes them look like big fat bellies!" Inge laughed, but she couldn't get him interested.

Ulrich, too, was trying to comfort Johannes and get him to think about things other than how he felt. Although he was no longer coughing as much, he clearly did not feel well and his chest congestion seemed to be getting worse rather than better.

❁　❁　❁

Many of the people they met at the shelter were on this ship, too. Most were now up on the deck, eager to see Rotterdam disappear in the distance, marking one more milestone along the way to Amerika.

Among them were the two Mennonite women who had given Barbara medicine for Johannes. Their husbands were with them and when they spotted the Holtzmanns standing by Jakob and Hans, they came over to them saying to the young shopkeepers, "We are Clara and Elisabeth, sisters married to brothers, Amos and Mathias Weber." They smiled at the children in their pleasant, friendly way and sat down with them.

The men immediately began talking about their plans in Amerika. Amos and Mathias were husky fellows, with sturdy shoes, large dark hats, and big work-roughened hands. "We are heading to the area called Lancaster Plain. It is part of western Chester County," Amos told Hans. "Some of our people are already there. They have been there since 1710. We plan to join them."

Jakob wanted to know what Amos and Mathias thought about business opportunities in Chester, "We were store keepers in Mosbach, and we hope to do that again. Do you know anything about those opportunities in the area where you are going?"

Mathias smiled and nodded his head. "There is probably a need for general stores everywhere, Jakob," he assured him. "If you like, I will ask when we meet our people in Philadelphia."

"Thank you, that is very nice of you," Jakob liked these men instantly. They were obviously fleeing the strict rule of the Swiss who had little love for the Anabaptist sects. How they were mistreated was common knowledge.

Ulrich felt like he couldn't concentrate on the conversation, because he, too, was getting more and more anxious about Johannes. He put his hand on Johannes' little forehead again, and thought to himself, "He is burning up!" Picking him up, he carried him down to the passenger deck.

There he found Barbara lying on a blanket in their sleeping area. She looked a bit sea sick from the movement of the boat. "I think Johannes is getting worse and he seems to have no energy," Ulrich told her. He touched the boy's head again.

Journey

"I noticed that earlier," Barbara replied, worry filled her voice. "I don't know what to do. He is so pale. I am afraid he won't be able to make this trip, Ulrich! He seems so sick; he won't eat or drink. We have barely begun the ocean voyage!"

"It only takes a day or so to get to Portsmouth or Cowes. If they think he has a serious illness, I am not sure what they will do with us." Ulrich's shoulders slumped as though he carried a great weight upon them. "I can't imagine they would send us back to Germany, but the ship won't want us and neither will the port if he has something contagious."

"Ulrich, see if you can find those two Mennonite sisters and ask if they know what we can do for him," Barbara asked. She felt like they seemed more knowledgeable than she was.

In moments, Ulrich returned with Clara and Elisabeth. Clara leaned down and put her ear to Johannes' chest; her eyes met Elisabeth's. "I think his chest congestion seems worse now than before." She looked up at Ulrich, "This can be quite serious in such a small boy."

"He needs hot broth, a cool bath, and a mustard plaster. I'm sorry to say, that will be difficult to get here," Elisabeth said thoughtfully. She was torn between alarming them and simply comforting them.

"I can make a mustard plaster, Elisabeth," said Clara. She hurried off to find the materials in her trunk.

"Thank you so much for coming down to give us your opinion," Barbara looked at them gratefully. She could see that Elisabeth was upset with Johannes' situation.

Clara returned with the mustard plaster which they applied to Johannes' chest. "I hope this will help him breathe better. I don't have all the ingredients, but we will do with what we have." She gently closed Johannes' shirt. "Prop his head up a bit," she said before they left him. "He has to breathe in the smell from the mixture to open his head and chest."

Ulrich's mind went back to the unfortunate family who had lost a son that cold night in the icy waters of the Neckar River. His very own words came rushing back to him - *"If they go back, they go back to the same things they were trying to escape, and they will have this terrible memory to live with. They have to bury him along the shore and go on."* Was he going to be able to follow his own advice and do that, he wondered.

After a few minutes, Ulrich stood up, a determined look on his face, "I am going to talk to the Captain. I think we need to get off in England. I know I can get a job with the shipbuilders. I can't risk my son!"

He went to the deck to find Thomas Martin.

Katja, who had just come down from the upper deck to check on her friend, heard the last part of the conversation. She came over to put her arm around Barbara. "If you leave us, I will miss you very much. Without you, it will just be me and the boys."

She tried to give Barbara encouragement, "Maybe in another year or two, you will be able to come to Amerika from here. I think life would be good in England for a skilled person like Ulrich."

Katja patted Barbara on the shoulder and turned to go up to deck again. She said quietly to herself, "Too far to go back, too far to go ahead. What a terrible decision!"

Twenty-Seven

THE NORTH SEA WIND took the *Good Queen* to the entrance of the Portsmouth Harbour in southern England, in about two day's travel. The port was located in an inlet protected from the ocean itself; there the water was calm. As the sailors were maneuvering the ship into the docking area, the captain called the passengers to the upper deck.

The passengers could see the green hills of England to the north. The wharf area was bustling with activity. The noise and smells from the city drifted across the water, beckoning them. Large warehouses, small shops, and homes were all mixed together in the area. Fishmongers were yelling out their wares, young children were running over the cobblestones playing a game of some sort, peddlers with hand carts were everywhere.

In his customary no-nonsense voice, Master Thomas Martin, using his interpreter, said, "We will be here a week or less, until we load mail and supplies for the colonies and get the royal permissions required for this voyage.

If you leave the ship, you will need permission from this officer, Mr. Worthington." He indicated the tall, slender Mr. Worthington standing like a servant beside him.

Thomas Martin continued, "There will be no meals served on board while we are in port. All must be on board an hour before sunset every day we are in Portsmouth."

Mr. Worthington stationed himself near the gangplank with his writing materials and papers. It was just about three hours until sunset, so he expected people would want fresh water, fruit and such from the market.

Ulrich hurried to the captain, hoping to talk with him while the interpreter was still at his side. "Sir, may I speak with you a moment?"

"I have business to attend at this moment. Not now," the ship's master answered sharply. He did not even look at Ulrich. Turning his back he began giving orders to some of the nearby sailors.

Ulrich was determined. He stayed right by the captain, never letting him out of his sight. Several times he said, "Sir, please, I need to talk with you."

Finally the ship was secure and the captain turned to his tormentor, crossed his arms, and barked, "WHAT do you want?"

Ulrich had talked to this kind of insolent authority many times in his life, so calmly and politely he answered, "My wife and I feel like we must cancel our plans to Amerika and stay here in Portsmouth. I am a carpenter by trade and I think there is work to be had here."

The captain's dark eyes took in this young German before him and thought he was probably telling the truth about staying and working, but he wasn't telling the truth about why. "Aren't you the one with the small boy who looked ill?"

Ulrich's heart skipped a beat as he answered, "Yes Sir." He was surprised that the captain could actually understand and speak limited German. Ulrich kept his words simple and clear, "My wife is afraid for him. Perhaps we will continue at another time."

"If you stay, the money for passage will not be refunded. You will have to speak with the immigration office for permission to stay and whether there is work to be had. They will not allow you to stay with no work." The captain's reply was gruff and uncaring.

"Where is the immigration office?" asked Ulrich.

"To the north, two streets over," the captain answered brusquely.

"Thank you, Sir." Ulrich hurried down to the passenger area to explain the situation to Barbara.

"If we stay, we lose the eight pounds passage money, and if we go we risk Johannes. How much money do we still have? Is it enough to do this?" Barbara was torn by this awful choice. She looked down at Johannes, who seemed to be worse with each passing minute.

"We will make do," Ulrich said. "It will be difficult, but if I get work quickly, it is possible. If I don't find work, we won't be allowed to stay. I think we should do it."

"Then first thing tomorrow, go to the office. Try to get permission to stay and find some work. If they say 'No' then we must continue on," Barbara sadly yielded to the forces beyond her control.

Twenty-Eight

THE MEIER FAMILY AND the Kramer brothers went to the market where they bought bread and some fried fish. Along with the fish was a white colored vegetable they had never seen before. It had been boiled in salted water.

"What is this?" Jorg said, holding a piece of the vegetable between his fingers.

"It looks like they peeled it and boiled it," Katja said as she tasted it. "Ummmm. It is good! I like it. Try it Jorg."

He took a tentative bite and smiled, "Ja. Gut!"

Wilhelm asked their Mennonite friends who had also come to the market with supper in mind, "Do you know this vegetable?"

"Ah, Ja, I have heard of it from our people in Amerika, but we do not yet have it in Switzerland. It is called potato."

"Is it common in Amerika?" Peter asked Amos. For the first time, he realized that farmers in Amerika may have

156

foods and equipment he was unfamiliar with or may not understand.

"My friends say the natives in Amerika knew of the potato. Spain has been selling them to the English and at the ports all along the Mediterranean."

Amos' brother Mathias surprised them when he added, "The Mennonites in Amerika raise them on their farms. They grow under the ground like carrots!"

"Maybe someday we will raise potatoes in Amerika," Peter laughed and lightly slapped the back of his brother Wilhelm. "We will have a new life!"

Jorg smiled, "Well, we have learned so much already -- all the different ships and now the potato!"

"Don't forget the shoes made of logs! And those things on Herr Hoogh's eyes!" shouted Inge laughing and making round circles with her fingers in front of her eyes.

Everyone laughed. It felt good to have met people whose company they enjoyed on this long journey.

Katja took a serving of fish and bread along back for Ulrich and Barbara, and a little potato for Johannes. "Barbara needs some cheering," she explained to Wilhelm when he questioned the extra food.

As they walked back to the boat, they noticed the things around them. "Ulrich should be here to see these houses with the wide wooden beams," Peter said.

They stopped for a few moments at a place where workmen were building a ship. Its frame was just beginning to take shape, giving a vision of what it would become.

Inge said, "It looks a chicken after all the meat is gone!" It made her laugh to think of it as a chicken.

"It does look like the skeleton of a really, really big chicken!" Jorg laughed. "Maybe it will lay eggs that will become little ships!" and the two of them got very silly over the thought.

Jakob and Hans stood and watched as the workmen, measured, cut, and carried lumber. Hans took Jorg by the hand, "When the boat is done and goes in the water, Jorg, the part that looks like a back bone will be the bottom."

Jorg was amazed. He tried to see this in his mind. "Do you think our ship looked like that once?"

"Probably," Hans smiled and nodded his head. As he worked with Jorg, he began to realize that he was a smart little boy also. Hans vowed that he would teach him to read all the way to Philadelphia.

Katja asked her brothers, "I heard Barbara and Ulrich talking about staying in England for a while, until Johannes is better. Do you think he could do this kind of work?"

They agreed Ulrich would be good at this. "We will tell

him to come down here tomorrow to find out if they can use another worker," Wilhelm said.

"I'm really sad to think he may not continue, but we must each do as we think we must," Peter commented with a touch of disappointment in his voice.

Twenty-Nine

THE NEXT MORNING ULRICH went immediately to the immigration office to ask permission to stay and work in the shipyard. He found the small office, located not far from the wharf. He opened the door and stepped into a single room with large windows which let in a lot of light. About six young men sat each at his own small, wooden desk, papers all around him. Some were working on figures, some were writing letters. Each was absorbed in his own work and glanced up only momentarily when he entered.

Ulrich approached the man he judged to be the oldest, thinking he may be the one in charge. "Sir, I would like to talk about staying in England to work in Portsmouth. I have come in on the *Good Queen* yesterday. I am a skilled carpenter."

The man got up, swished his long-tailed coat back in place, and straightened his collar. Without a smile, said flatly, "English?"

Ulrich was at a disadvantage, but thought he was asking his nationality, so he replied, "German."

The man, a skinny fellow, with his long hair pulled back and tied with a bow, repeated the same word, "English?"

One of the younger men got up from his desk and came over to Ulrich. He said in German, "Do you speak English?"

Ulrich shook his head, "Nein."

The younger man looked at Ulrich, noticing he had the rough hands of a laborer; he had heard him say he was a carpenter looking for work in the shipyard. He turned to the older man and explained.

"Does he understand British measure?" the older man asked. "Tell him we don't need more German peasants with no skills and no money! We have plenty of them already crowding our poorhouses."

Again the young man, who said his name was Geoffry, turned and asked Ulrich about the British measure. He graciously did not add the last comment.

"Nein," Ulrich replied. His shoulders began to sag a bit. He had had such high hopes for this. "I will learn. I understand the local measure where I lived. It can't be so hard to learn this. I have much experience! I am a good carpenter from a family of good carpenters! I have built many things."

The young man, gave a flat, business-like smile, shook his head, and said, "I am sorry, we only hire those who are familiar with British measure and we have no shortage of workers. We do prefer English speaking. Good Day, Sir." He turned and went back to his work desk.

The older man ignored Ulrich and sat down to his own work, his back toward the door.

Ulrich stood for a moment looking at the men, all of whom now had their heads bent to their own tasks once more. He felt very much unwanted and out of place. He thought, "Why do people who have so much, care so little about others?" He turned and walked slowly, sadly, out the door.

This meant they would go on, just like that family on the Neckar River. He felt defeated.

Thirty

ULRICH ARRIVED BACK ON the ship to find Johannes much worse. He didn't even tell Barbara about his experience in the immigration office. She was upset enough.

Ulrich sat down beside Barbara and stroked the back of his little son lying in his mother's arms. He realized he was going to lose his precious child. By evening, even the Mennonite sisters, Elisabeth and Clara, could see Johannes' struggle to breathe would be lost.

Barbara never left him, she held him close, trying to keep his head up to make his breathing easier, but it was to no avail. She sang to him quietly as she had always done.

"Walk outside a bit, I'll take him," Ulrich urged.

"No, he is going to die in his mother's arms," she said sadly, and stayed right where she was. In the night she felt him relax and simply quit breathing. Quietly he was gone.

Just like Grandfather, they wrapped him a piece of sailcloth and buried him without a stone in the corner of the nearest churchyard. It was a very sad day.

Their Mennonite friends, said a prayer at the gravesite and read from their German Bible. Then they walked slowly, sadly, back to the ship where Barbara went down to the passenger deck and sat by their trunk with her head in her hands. The sadness of leaving her only child in an unmarked grave, in the cold earth of a foreign land, was too much for her.

Finally, Katja came to her, "Come on up to the deck with me and sit in the sunshine. It will make you feel better." She took Barbara's hand and led her to the deck.

Thirty-One

THE LAST TWO DAYS in Portsmouth Harbour, were sunny and bright. April was drawing to a close. Katja tried to coax Barbara to come on shore and walk through the market. "The days on the sea will be long, let's enjoy this now."

In spite of Katja's efforts, Barbara was depressed from the loss of her son, and rarely went off the ship except to walk to the unmarked spot where he lay in the churchyard. There she knelt on the freshly disturbed soil and sobbed for the young boy who would lie alone so far from his homeland, so far from his mother.

Katja and Hans and Jakob took Inge and Jorg exploring in the fields just at the edge of town. The children loved the walks, for it reminded them of home. The brothers went along, too, if they couldn't find a small job that day.

"I think I have met almost everyone on this ship," Hans said. "There is a shoemaker, at least three carpenters, several blacksmiths, a weaver and many farmers!"

Jacob laughed, "Hans, you could strike up a conversation with a stump!" He knew it took only two days for Hans to find out something about everyone on board. He was the extrovert.

"You are the outgoing one, brother, - the talker of the group! I only met one other shopkeeper," Jakob said. "He told me he is going to stay in Philadelphia with his uncle." He looked at Hans, " I think we should consider going to this area in Chester County, called Lancaster Plain, where Amos and Mathias are headed. We could open a shop there. I think they would give us some good advice about where to locate."

Hans chuckled. Typical of business-minded Jakob, he was already planning how they could get started in Amerika and they hadn't even begun to cross the sea!

Hans turned to Katja, "Where will you go when your older brothers are redeemed?"

"I don't know," Katja replied. Now that they were only a few months from their destination, the future for the youngest members of the family began to trouble her. Her expression showed more than she wanted to tell. "I am hoping whoever redeems Peter and Wilhelm will have a job for me, or maybe they will have friends who need a cook or a maid."

"What about Inge and Jorg?" For some reason Hans couldn't explain, he began to worry about how Katja would take care of the little ones on her own. He imagined that she may have to beg for food on the street.

He stopped and took her shoulders, turning her toward him. Looking into her pretty face he said, "Did you ever think of marrying?"

She smiled up at him, a little surprised at the question. "Several times my brothers tried to arrange for me to do that, but I felt that I needed to take care of Inge and Jorg. They have no one else."

Then she added, "They wouldn't force me to marry someone I didn't want to marry." The thought of marrying Hans was something she hadn't considered; she had always thought of him as a good friend.

He grinned that winning grin of his and said, "Well, a shopkeeper needs wife you know, and children, too." Then he added devilishly, "To carry all the things and do the work while he runs about the countryside!"

Peter heard that last comment and laughed, "That is why Wilhelm and I chased away all her suitors! Who would cook for us and do the work?"

"That's right, we sent the geese to chase them away!" Wilhelm laughed at his own joke.

Katja kept her eyes on Hans as he spoke. She thought to herself, he really is a good person. She took his hand and said, "It is an idea to consider, Hans. You've always been a good friend." For the first time she really began to consider this.

❀　❀　❀

On the last day at Portsmouth Harbour, they ate the evening meal at the marketplace. This could be the last fresh fruit and greens they would have for a few months.

The friends each had an English beer. "One thing for sure, the English could learn about how to make beer from the Germans!" said Peter, swinging his mug and finishing the last of it. "This stuff would choke Grandfather!"

They took boiled eggs and cheese back to the ship, where they watched the sun descend for the last time on this side of the ocean. It filled them at once with excitement and apprehension.

The Atlantic

Thirty-Two

Just as the light of early dawn began to illuminate the steps to the passenger deck, they felt the ship moving out of the inlet as it headed toward the Atlantic. Before the day was done they expected to be out of sight of England and the journey across the ocean would have begun.

The passengers, sat up on their blankets when they felt the ship's movement. Many got up and went up to the deck to watch the *Good Queen* sail past the Isle of Wight and into the English Channel, then turn west toward open sea.

When the ship was underway, the sailors brought them biscuits and a jug of water which Katja divided for the family, pouring some into each brother's cup. Then she carefully stowed the remainder in a spot where it would not tip over. Taking their cup and biscuit, they went to sit on the upper deck where the fresh air was a relief from the stuffiness below.

Katja stood at the railing and tried to breathe deeply, clearing her lungs. "It certainly gets stuffy down there!"

"Do you think I will ever get used to sleeping wrapped in blanket without the straw ticking of home?" groaned Peter, stretching his back to get the kinks out of it. He felt sore and a bit grumpy.

"I just wish I could stretch my whole body out. I feel as though I am rolled up like a meat dumpling!" complained Wilhelm.

It wasn't long until most of the other passengers had come up on deck, too. Amos and Mathias came up with their group and introduced some of them to the brothers and their friends. "We are mostly farmers, " Amos said, "Rufus, here, is a carpenter, and Christian is a preacher," he touched each on the sleeve as he introduced them. "We have Obediah, who is a cooper, and Philip, a wonderful baker. They all have wives and some have children with them," Mathias added, waving his hand toward their families, "except handsome Hansel, here. He is yet unmarried."

Amos put his arm around Hansel, pretending a secret, he said in a very loud whisper, "I think the elders have a plan for Hansel. We are told there are some pretty girls in our Lancaster group looking for a husband!" Hansel smiled a shy smile which made him look boyish and appealing.

Katja thought he was certainly handsome, but he looked younger than her brother Peter, very young to marry. She could see the Mennonites were a close group who took care of each other. She thought to herself, "Just like Wilhelm, Peter, and I." She felt a camaraderie with them.

Wilhelm and Jakob could see the children playing on the other side of ship. Inge and Jorg had joined them and seemed to be having no trouble with the rolling waves and the movement of the ship.

Wilhelm was having no such luck with the undulating waves. He said, "I don't know if I could be a sailor. I am starting to feel a bit sick already. I am not even out of site of land!" He sat down on the floor beside Ulrich and Barbara, both of whom looked a little pallid.

"It is probably better to be here in the fresh air," Wilhelm groaned and leaned his head back, putting his unfinished biscuit in his empty cup. He sat that way for hours, trying to talk himself out of being seasick.

Peter and Hans walked around through the passengers introducing themselves and chatting with everyone. They stopped beside one man who stood looking over the side of the ship in an effort to relocate the large fish he thought he saw in the distance. His wife was by his side trying to follow his direction. "Where are you headed in America?" Hans asked him.

He turned to Hans, "I am a printer. We are going to Germantown. Her brother is a taylor there." The two of them were large people, dressed better than most on this trip. Peter could see she was pregnant.

"I am Nicholaus and this is Anna. We have an eight year old son around here somewhere." He cast his eyes over the deck but did not see him. "And, my Anna may have another here on the ship!" He put his huge arm around her and gave her a hug.

❁   ❁   ❁

The farther from land they got, the more the *Good Queen* tossed in the heavy sea. Before the first week had passed more than half of the adult passengers were seasick, dragging themselves up onto the main deck only to lie there in the hope that the fresh air would revive them. They lay without moving, looking like soldiers on a battlefield.

The sailors ignored them except to tell them to stay back out of the way of their work. The seamen knew from experience that a few passengers would die quickly from the complications of seasickness.

Very quickly the passenger area had become uncomfortable. The smell of chamber buckets, and vomit filled the windowless, crowded space so that the air there was stifling. Already the rolling sea and the rations were beginning to take a toll on some.

Katja noticed that there were some on board who were so sick, they were unable to drink water or keep down even a bite of food. She thought to herself, at least Wilhelm is getting better and is eating and walking around a bit.

Thirty-Three

A LITTLE MORE THAN two weeks out, on fifteenth of May, they ran into a gale with very strong winds and heavy rain. The passengers spotted it on the horizon - a terrifying black-cloud bearing down on them like an oncoming menace. When it reached them, water poured down into the passenger area in torrents soaking everyone near the gangway. The wind blew in adding cold to the wetness. Everyone tried to move over a bit, but there was nowhere to go in the crowded conditions. Each was trapped in his own small space, trying unsuccessfully to stay dry and warm.

Katja noticed one of the passengers, the butcher from Freiburg, appeared to be very sick. His wife sat by him saying, "Just relax, Rutger. Lie still and rest." She put her hand on his warm forehead. "Little, Rudi, go get this cloth wet to lay on Papa's head." She handed her son a cloth which he took to the steps and made it wet.

Seeing her difficulties, Katja made her way across the room to the wife, Maria. It was obvious to Katja even at a distance that she, too, was worn out from the strain of being caretaker while ill herself.

"What do you think is wrong with him?" Katja asked her. She looked down at the butcher, Rutger Bauman, a large, muscular man lying like a helpless child with his head on his wife's lap. Up close, as Katja studied Maria's face she could see the woman was just as sick as her husband, flushed and exhausted looking.

"Ah, the food doesn't agree with us," Maria declared. "He is sick from it. We are used to eating good fresh meat! He has been sick since we reached the open sea!"

She wiped her eyes and looked up at Katja, lines of fatigue clearly showing in her face. "I think my youngest child, Elke, and I are getting this sickness, too. She hasn't eaten for a week either. The salt pork is giving Rutger and I the flux. I haven't gotten any rest for two days! We can't eat or keep even water down!"

Elisabeth, Katja's friend, came over to help and suggested, "Maybe we could put out a bowl and catch some rain water for him to drink. It would be better than this water from the wooden kegs." She hurried to her trunk and got a bowl which she put where the rain would fill it. In a short time she had a little water for him. "Here," she said, putting it gently to his lips, "try to drink this."

He tried but Katja could see he was getting worse before her eyes. The one swallow he did get down, came right back up. With Rutger's head on her lap, Maria held her limp looking, two year old, Elke, in her arms. Katja threw a blanket over her shoulders and realized there was nothing else she could do.

The storm lasted two days and two nights, tossing the ship and drenching the passengers. By the time they had passed through it, Rutger Bauman, his wife, Maria, and their youngest daughter were all dead from dysentery and dehydration.

They were the first to be buried at sea. The hearts of the passengers went out to the two remaining children holding on to each other as they watched the rolling waves claim the bodies of their parents, leaving them alone and on their own.

The burial set a sad and solemn tone for all as they realized how narrow was the line that separated life from death.

Katja and Peter came and sat beside the two remaining Bauman children. She put her arm around the girl. "Do you know if your parents were meeting someone in Philadelphia?" she asked them. Rudi, ten years, and his sister, Magdalena, eight years, sat stunned from the loss of their parents. They could only shake their heads.

Finally, Rudi managed to say, "I think Papa was going to try to find a butcher in Philadelphia who would hire him. He wanted to have his own shop someday like the one he had back in Freiburg."

"Do you know anyone in Philadelphia?" Katja asked him

gently. She could feel Magdalena trembling in her arms, making quiet little sobs.

"Nein, no one," Rudi said sadly. He turned his head and looked into Katja's face, his eyes betraying his fear, "What will happen to us?"

"Do you know if your father paid his fare or if he was going to be redeemed?" asked Peter who was concerned about the two orphans.

"I am sure they paid," Rudi said. "They have some money in the trunk."

Peter put his arm around the child, and spoke into his ear, "Don't tell anyone else that, Rudi, it will be our secret."

Rudi understood immediately and nodded his head, thankful that Peter had told him something he hadn't thought of himself.

"Stay by us here on the ship. We will keep an eye on you until we get to Philadelphia," Katja said. She knew she could not help them more than that, but her heart went out to the orphans. Whatever would happen to two children alone in a strange city, in a strange land?

Thirty-Four

ABOUT A WEEK LATER, Master Thomas Martin brought the passengers to the deck to make a short announcement. Standing before them in his blue and white uniform he gave the appearance of authority. In his customarily dictatorial voice he stated, "Today, I, Thomas Martin, Master of the *Good Queen*, announce that on this day, 24 May, 1720, we have reached the half-way point on this voyage. According to the rules agreed upon prior to this voyage, the fees for any person aboard this ship who is planning to be redeemed at the port of Philadelphia must be paid by his kin in the event that he should die at sea." Without further comment, Captain Martin turned on his heel and disappeared into his chart house.

The passengers stood silently for a few moments. None of them remembered such a rule agreed upon back in Rotterdam. They looked at each other and finally, they began to ask their companions, "What does that mean?"

One man, a baker from Erfurt, spoke up. "I have heard

about this, but I do not remember seeing it on the Rotterdam papers. It means you must redeem yourself for several extra years to pay for a deceased spouse or sibling." He was obviously furious --his voice loud, his face flushed, his eyes dark with anger. "I think he is dishonest. We are certainly not halfway in a few weeks!"

Another angry passenger, the Darmstadt weaver, spoke up in support of his fellow voyager, "Who knows something about sailing? I don't think we are half way, we have not been out of Portsmouth even four weeks!" His face showed his disbelief. He was a husky fellow who waved his arms in the air as he spoke.

The passengers were beginning to get visibly agitated. "I think he is lying!" shouted a woman. "He is trying to trick us, to make more money for himself!" She, too, shook her fist in the captain's direction, even though he had gone into the chart house and couldn't see her.

A younger woman standing nearby said quietly, "He doesn't care what you think. He knows we are helpless in this matter. "

"Ja, you are right!" said her husband, with a note of hopelessness in his voice, "Like a prisoner threatening the jailer through the air vent!"

"Let's make him show us his charts!" shouted the shoemaker from Karlsruhe who started to walk in the same direction the captain had gone. Several more started to move en masse with him.

A large, heavy set man from Mannheim, whom they knew to be Gerhardt Dietrich, stood up and raised his hands above his head. He lifted his voice and shouted, "Wait! We don't have anyone among us who can read the Captain's charts. He has the power here. Let us think this over before we make the rest of the voyage more miserable than it is already." His coat was blowing in the slight breeze, but his voice was the voice of calm reason.

A tall man, a blacksmith from Basel, agreed with Herr Dietrich saying, "We can make a complaint about him in Philadelphia if we still think this is true!"

"I will write this in a log for the record," Dietrich assured them. The passengers knew that back in Germany, Dietrich had been a town official, so they halted their march to the captain. They realized Herr Dietrich was right, they were without power on this issue. As one, they turned and went back toward their area somewhat deflated, exchanging ideas about this with their companions their angry words fading away in the wind as they walked .

Jakob, who stood watching this was shaking his head with disbelief, "It is hard to believe that Captain Martin would behave like this!"

"Everyone is not honest and kind like you," Wilhelm said keeping his voice low, "I have met many greedy ones like him. They will do anything to benefit themselves and nothing for you."

Peter added, "Just because he is the ship's Master, doesn't mean you can trust him or even believe him!"

Sensing a body pressing against him, Peter realized that Rudi and Magdalena, the deceased butcher's orphans, were beside him. A small hand pulled on his shirt, "Peter, does that mean that we must pay more for Mama and Papa and little Elke?" Their eyes reflected their fear.

Peter put his arm around them trying to calm them. "No, you said your Mama and Papa paid for the tickets. The Captain means that people like Wilhelm and I would have to pay with extra years if something happened to one of us after the ship was halfway. Don't worry, we won't let him do that to you."

The two children breathed a sigh of relief and stayed close to the brothers for the rest of the day.

As people started to disburse, Magdalena whispered to her brother, "Rudi, what will happen to us? We have no one to show us the way. We know nothing about Philadelphia! I am afraid! People can tell us anything and we won't know if it is true or not!"

"Don't be afraid, Magdalena, we will figure something out. There are some nice families here, they will give us advice." He tried to sound much more sure and confident than he really felt. He didn't want to tell her that he, too, was afraid and worried what would become of them.

Thirty-Five

ON THE SECOND DAY of June, Nicholaus, the printer who was going to Germantown, hurried over to Katja. In a very excited voice, he said, "Come quickly, please! Anna is going to have her baby! Now! Her water has broken!"

Katja grabbed Barbara's hand and said, "Come, I need you to help me. Get Elisabeth and Clara, and come to Nicholaus and Anna. Hurry!"

Katja turned to Jorg, "See if you can get the sailors to give you a jug of water."

By the time Katja got over to Anna, she was well on her way to giving birth. Katja had nothing to spread out on the blanket for cleanliness; she had nothing to offer for pain like the special tea they used back home. Having a baby in these crowded conditions made a difficult experience much worse.

Katja stroked Anna's face and arms trying to keep her calm as she lay suffering with pain. Katja pushed the hair from her sweating face, and spoke to her in a quiet voice.

Somehow, Jorg returned with an extra jug of water which he got from the ship's surgeon, who refused to come and help. He had waved Jorg away saying, "Poor Germans are not my problem. I only tend the sailors."

Elisabeth and Clara were able to find a few large pieces of cloth which they placed under her. The four women shooed Nicholaus back a bit and surrounded Anna with their bodies, forming a circle, trying to give her at least a minimum of privacy. Real privacy was impossible. Anna lay on her blanket sweating and straining. Each contraction brought with it a cry of pain.

Barbara held her hand. "Hold on to me, Anna. Push. Breathe. Push. Just make as much noise as you want."

"At least this one is coming easier than the first," groaned Anna trying to smile, then another wave of pain came, pushing with it another loud cry from her lips. She squeezed Barbara's hand.

"Keep trying, Anna," Barbara and Katja encouraged her as still another wave of pain struck. "The pains are very close. That is good sign, Anna. It will be soon now."

Another great pain and then the top of the head could be seen. Within the next few minutes, Anna had a new baby girl with a lusty voice of her own -- the first birth on the journey.

"We will take care of the mother," Elisabeth and Clara said to Katja and Barbara. "We are good at this and have done it many times."

They handed the newborn to Katja and Barbara. "You two take care of the new daughter."

"Ohhhh…,"Barbara sighed as she cradled the sticky, wet newborn while Katja tried to wash her with a wet cloth. A woman nearby handed them a clean, warm blanket to wrap around baby.

Katja watched as Barbara cradled the new baby in her arms, holding it close, giving it the warmth of her own body. She could tell that holding this squealing, new life helped Barbara make a step past the loss of her own little one. She smiled as the infant howled and kicked its arms and legs.

Elisabeth and Clara were as skilled in midwifery as their word. It was not long until they announced, "Anna is ready to receive her new daughter. The mother seems to be doing well."

"Here, Anna, is your beautiful daughter," Barbara said as she laid the baby on its mother's belly.

Katja looked at Nicholaus, who had watched anxiously from a few steps back. "Come greet your new daughter, Nicholaus."

"I am so thankful to see my little girl and my beautiful wife both healthy and well," he beamed. "I was very worried in these conditions." His big hand reached out and gently touched the head of the infant in a gesture of fatherly love. He kissed Anna on the cheek and whispered something in her ear.

Elisabeth told Anna, "Our friend, Christian Guttmann, will come to you. He is a preacher with our group and he can write a paper for you about the birth of your daughter." She went off looking for Christian.

When he arrived, Christian said. "I have brought my pen and paper. This is one of the best parts of the ministry in my opinion." He smiled as though the baby were his own.

Leaning his pen and paper on the Schaeffer trunk, he said, "I will write: *The daughter of Nicholaus and Anna Schaeffer is born on 2 June, 1720 aboard the ship the Good Queen on its way to Amerika from England.*" Looking up at them, pen paused in a way that wouldn't make ink drops on the precious paper, he asked, "Do you know what you will name her?"

"We will name her Maria Isabele, the name of Anna's mother," said Nicholaus. "It is our custom."

Christian wrote: *This daughter of Nicholaus and Anna is named Maria Isabele*. He blotted the paper so that it was completely dry and handed it to Nicholaus. "May she be blessed," he smiled.

Nicholaus took the paper and put it in their trunk for safe keeping.

Thirty-Six

NEAR THE END OF June, the *Good Queen* gave the passengers their first taste of an early hurricane which had blown out to sea from the east coast of Amerika. The sky was ominously dark; winds of extreme magnitude tossed the ship as though it were a child's toy. Waves grew bigger than any of the passengers had ever imagined possible.

They huddled in semi-darkness of the passenger section and looked out the entrance as the rain poured down in sheets of water. None of the passengers had ever experienced this kind of storm which the sailors called a hurricane. It was much worse than the gale they had experienced earlier on the voyage.

"At times it seems like we are nearly vertical," shouted Jakob over the wind, as he tried to hold on to the little ones whose small, light bodies were easily tossed around.

"Watch out, Jorg!" Katja cried as one of the heavy trunks began to slide toward him threatening to crush him against the side of the ship. He moved quickly to her side, terrified.

Putting his hand into the little purse around his neck, Jorg wrapped his fingers around Grandfather's stone. The cool smoothness of it calmed him as he felt Grandfather's spirit reassuring him that this would pass and he would be safe.

The strong wind, the wet slippery floor, the constantly changing, wild angles of the boat on the waves, the sliding objects made the bravest heart palpitate, filling one with dread. Children were screaming, chamber buckets were sloshing over their rim. Some people were praying, some were calling out in fright, "God, save us!" Everything was getting soaked from the rain which poured in torrents down the gangway.

Families clung to each other. The two trembling orphans came and without a word sat on the floor close by Ulrich who put an arm around each of them.

One of the other children, a boy of about six years, became so frightened, he began screaming and kicking his legs wildly. He struggled loose from his father's grip and ran toward the gangway.

Everyone was in shock, "Stop! Don't go out!" The ones nearest the entrance tried to reach him, but the confusion and the heaving floor of the ship made it impossible.

The child was up the two or three steps to the deck before

anyone could stop him, shrieking, "Let me out! ... Let me out!"

Slipping and sliding, his father struggled after him yelling, "Stop, Karl! Stop!"

The moment child reached the deck, the tremendous hurricane winds picked up his small body from the slippery boards and tossed him into the heaving sea.

Without thinking the father jumped in after him in an effort to save him. They were both immediately swallowed up in the tumult.

"I have never been so frightened!" Barbara cried. She was shaking and wet from head to toe

"I am wet and cold, too," Ulrich shouted over the noise. He realized he had his arms around the two orphans, in a near death grip. He looked down into their frightened faces, "Are you alright?"

They nodded, frightened, but comforted by his arms as they sat huddled together on the wet floor.

"I understand why the little boy was terrified. He wanted this to stop! He wanted to run away from it. This is like some kind of torture!" Rudi said.

The storm lasted into the night. Everyone clung together for stability and comfort.

Finally, with the dawn, the sea began to calm; the morning light enabled passengers to see the damage. The rain had passed over; the sun began to appear among the quickly dissipating clouds. People began to stand up and move around.

Hans looked around the room, "Everything is soaked. Trunks are everywhere. Let's see if we can lift up our blankets and try to get them outside on the deck." He reached down and began to pick up the blankets at his feet. Peter and Wilhelm helped him.

Most of the people had the same idea. Everyone was gathering up the bedding which had been soaked by the sloshing chamber buckets and soiled with the vomit of sickened passengers. The sailors brought up tubs of sea water to rinse the smelly blankets which were then carefully laid out to dry in the emerging sun.

"There is one good thing about this," Wilhelm said to Peter as they sloshed the blankets up and down in the tubs of salt water.

"Whatever could that be?" Peter wondered.

"The salt water might kill the lice that are chewing me to bits!"

"You are right about that, brother!" Peter agreed. "I want to get into this tub of sea water myself."

Katja arrived with more dirty blankets. "Who was the child who ran out the door in the middle of the storm?" she asked them.

"I think there were just the two of them," Hans answered. "I talked to the father one day and he told me the mother died last year while giving birth to a sister who also died. He and his son were going to start over in Amerika."

"How very sad," said Katja. She knew what it was to be so afraid, that she wanted to run.

Thirty-Seven

As they finished spreading the blankets in the sun and walked back toward the stairs, a very frightened Rudi ran up to them. "Help me," he cried taking Ulrich by the sleeve. "A man is trying to get into our trunk."

Hans and Ulrich dashed down into the disordered mess of the passenger deck behind Rudi. There they found a stocky, muscular fellow shaking the trunk in an effort to get it open.

"Stop! What are you doing?" demanded Hans putting both hands on the trunk forcing it to the floor.

The fellow looked up, surprised to be confronted. "This is my trunk. I am trying to get it open. The water has got it rusted shut!" He was dirty and ragged, as they all were by now.

"That is not your trunk!" shouted Hans. "It belongs to Rudi, here."

"I am in charge of him, now. He asked me to take care of

his trunk!" lied the fellow. He put his fists on his hips, his feet spread apart in a fighting stance.

"He is not in charge of me. I don't even know him!" shouted Rudi sticking out his chest, trying to look tough in his young boy way.

It was obvious to Ulrich that this man was trying to take advantage of these orphans. It filled him with anger. "He is with us!" stated Ulrich firmly. "Go away from here and let these children alone."

Hans and Ulrich had the same idea at once. They reached down, picked up the trunk, and moved it over with their own.

"Do you know him?" asked Ulrich who put his arm around Rudi after they had placed the trunk in a new location.

Rudi shook his head, "He has been watching us, but he is not with us. It was just our family, there was no one else. I told Magdalena not to talk to him, not to answer his questions."

"Well, you stay over here with us now. You will be safe here," Ulrich patted him on the shoulder. "It was good the trunk was locked. Do you know where the key is in this mess?"

Rudi smiled and reached inside his shirt. He held up the key on a leather strip around his neck. "Papa gave it to me when we got on board. He told me not to take it off -- ever!"

"Good!" Ulrich told him. "Keep it right there."

Thirty-Eight

By late afternoon most blankets were dry and back in place, trunks had been set up again, and things were getting back to normal.

Two husky sailors came down to the passenger deck. The biggest one announced, "There was a man who jumped overboard yesterday in the storm by the name of Frederich Schneider. Where is his trunk?"

"Why do you want to know?" Gerhardt Dietrich asked. He was probably the only one on board who was not afraid of Captain Martin or his sailors.

"We are taking it to the captain. He ordered us to bring it," the other sailor growled. "It is not your business, Dietrich. Don't stand in the way!" The sailor with the scarf-like belt around his waist gave him a shove.

But Dietrich was not to be controlled. "Has Herr Schneider no heirs?" he asked, his voice growing louder.

"What does it matter to you? The trunk belongs to the

captain now," the sailors told him. The two of them were getting irritated with the bossy passenger, Dietrich.

"We told you," the other sailor said loudly, backing up his partner, "the man died, his things belong to the captain."

"Don't you have that wrong? Don't you mean the captain steals the dead man's belongings?" Dietrich took a step closer to the sailors.

"Be quiet, Dietrich. We'll put you in punishment!" The heavier sailor shook his fist at the passenger.

"Suppose he has money in his trunk," insisted Dietrich, "or valuables."

"Not your business, Dietrich! Don't argue with Master Martin. You will find yourself in trouble!"

Fearful that this would turn into a brawl, one of the more easily frightened passengers, pointed silently to Frederich Schneider's trunk. The sailors picked it up and were quickly gone up to the top deck.

"Even if he had heirs, they would never know about his trunk," growled Dietrich shaking with anger. "They keep anything of value for themselves -- sort of like the spoils of war."

Wilhelm got up and went over to Dietrich, "Don't get all upset by it, Gerhardt. You can't win with his kind. Believe me, we know."

"We certainly do know his kind," added Peter. "Why do you think we are all trying to find a new life in Amerika?"

"When *I* get to Amerika," declared Gerhardt Dietrich, "I am going to dedicate myself to correcting these evils!" He tramped off to his own blanket.

Thirty-Nine

On the first day July, Katja and Barbara, sat on the deck with the two Mennonite sisters, Elisabeth and Clara, enjoying the warm morning sun.

Barbara said, "I never imagined that we would have delivered three more babies since Anna's little Isabele!"

"Ja, it is unfortunate that only Anna and little Isabele survived the struggle of birth under the ship's conditions," said Elisabeth sadly.

"I shall never forget those mothers buried at sea with their babes wrapped in their arms," Katja remembered sadly. "Thank Heaven for your Mennonite preacher, Christian, who led a prayer and a hymn as they were lowered into the sea. We needed him to do that."

Barbara added, "Although most on board are Lutherans not Mennonites, we are grateful to you. We are united in the effort to survive, if not in religious practice."

Elisabeth answered, "Pennsylvania is a place of religious tolerance, we begin on this ship."

"It is so sad, to have come so far and be so close, but not make it," Barbara commented. "The ones who are left, blame themselves, I'm sure."

"How well we know," Ulrich put his arm around Barbara as he joined the ladies in sun. The two of them sat beside each other watching the two orphans who were playing a game with Jorg on the other side of the ship.

Ulrich interrupted her thoughts when he turned to Barbara and asked, "Barbara, could you bring yourself to adopt the two orphans, Rutger and Magdalena?" He hesitated, then added, "This has been on my mind since I saw the fear on their faces during the last storm."

Elated, Barbara looked at him in surprise, "I have thought about it, myself. It seems like we have been put here for them, doesn't it?" She took Ulrich's hand.

"When I saw the fear on their faces, I was touched. We are in a position to do something," Ulrich told her. His eyes never left her face. "Let's think about it and talk with them."

Barbara felt good when she realized that she and Ulrich were of the same mind about the orphans.

She thought, Rudi and Magdalena were children alone without parents; she knew that she and Ulrich needed to step into this void. She realized it had taken her weeks to get over the death of Johannes, but now she understood, she must go on. They needed to do that, too.

Barbara was filled with happiness when Ulrich approached Gerhardt Dietrich to ask his advice.

Gerhard's reply was, "I will write for you a paper which verifies that their parents died on this voyage and they are orphans with no known relatives in Amerika. I will also write that you have agreed to take them as your own and care for them. They are not redemptioners."

Ulrich signed the paper; Barbara made her mark. She was pleasantly surprised when both Rutger and Magdalena said, "We know how to write our own names! Papa insisted that we learn this." They proudly showed off their skill as they wrote their names on bottom of the page that would change their lives forever.

Forty

"If we don't soon get to Amerika, we'll all be too weak from hunger to work!" Peter said, his hand on his stomach. "The food is terrible, and all that good cheese and dried fruit we brought along has been gone long ago!"

"I think today is the first of July," Jakob noted. "The ship's provisions must be getting very low. We left England the first week of May! We are surely close to our destination."

"Food quality was never wonderful, but now it seems less quantity *and* quality!" complained Peter. "I would almost swim back to Heidelberg for a boiled cabbage or a fresh sausage like the one we had at the Wurstkuche in Heidelberg!"

"I saw a man catch a rat yesterday," remarked Hans. "Do you think he was going to eat it?" He rolled his eyes at his brother and made a face.

"Yes, I do! There are plenty of them on board this ship,"

answered Jakob. He felt his stomach turn at the thought. "I hear them at night scrambling around in the cargo deck."

Jakob looked over at Amos and Mathias, their Mennonite friends, who were standing nearby and heard the conversation. "What do you think, fellows?"

"When we get to Philadelphia, keep an eye out for our people who will come out to the ship with fresh food. They wrote to us that they would do that when they know we are at the wharf," Amos smiled.

"We will look forward to that!" Jakob said. "I am ready to eat about anything that comes along! I am sick of salt pork, porridge, and hard, wormy biscuits! Even the water tastes terrible!"

Just then, Captain Martin called everyone to the top deck. "Tomorrow we will see the coast of North Amerika, and soon we'll enter the Delaware Bay. From there we will travel up the Delaware River for several days to Philadelphia, stopping at night and traveling in the daylight." As was his custom, he took no questions and returned to his chart room.

Smiles of relief were everywhere; everyone was pleased with the announcement. People lingered on deck standing in small groups speaking with each other about their plans in Amerika.

"Thank Heaven!" Ulrich remarked to Barbara as each

kept an arm around Rudi and Magdalena who were beside them.

Rudi spoke up, "Magdalene and I are so happy that we will land in Philadelphia with the two of you as our parents!"

"We were both very much afraid. Now we can look forward to our new life!" agreed Magdalene.

Ulrich told the man who stood near him, "We plan to stay in Philadelphia where I hope to find carpenter work. "Gerhardt Dietrich told us that Philadelphia is the biggest city in America with almost twenty thousand people!"

"Really!" the man was surprised. "There certainly must be work there for your kind of carpenter skills!"

"People here need such things as furniture and small carriage buildings. I know I can find work." Ulrich agreed."Even though it scares Barbara that we do not know the customs or the language, I am looking forward to our new beginning now."

Barbara, who was glad to be a mother again, smiled happily at her expanded family.

Jorg and Inge were playing on deck with the other children. Inge came running over to Barbara shouting excitedly, "Look! Birds! Do you see the birds!" She was twirling around with her hands reaching toward the sky, her golden curls bouncing in the breeze. Even in her ship-worn, dirty clothes, she was the picture of joy dancing across the deck!

The children seemed to sense that the birds were a good sign.

"You are right! What a welcome sight!" Barbara laughed out loud. She was certainly happy for the sign of land.

Katja, standing nearby, turned and let her eyes wander skyward where the seabirds glided, looking so carefree. Momentarily she thought what it might be like to spread her wings and fly away. Now that the end of the voyage seemed near, another problem had begun to weigh on her mind: how would she cope with the two small children and her big brothers somewhere else. It would be difficult for a young woman alone with two small children to feed and clothe. She remembered Hans' comment …'a shopkeeper needs a wife and children, too.' Maybe she should take him up on the offer of marriage. Things were going to be different here in Amerika. She would have to make a new life, too.

She needed to talk to Wilhelm and Peter about this very soon. She saw them sitting over on the starboard side with their heads bent together in deep conversation.

As she walked near them, she could hear Wilhelm say, "If we get split up and are redeemed by different people, we must have someone write a name and place for each of us so we can meet there."

"The only people we know here who have a definite destination is Amos and Mathias. We need their location because we can meet in that area," suggested Peter. "We don't really know any area in this new country."

"That is a good idea," Wilhelm brightened at the idea of having a way to contact each other in a completely unfamiliar land. Even though he was the older one, he couldn't remember a time when Peter was not by his side. Thoughtfully, he sighed, "Oye! Such changes are in store for us!"

"I am anxious to get started, so that our redemption time will be finished in five summers. Then we can meet and start our own lives," Peter said. "I want us to be back together as soon as we have worked off our fees."

Forty-One

KATJA SAT DOWN BESIDE her brothers, her outward appearance alerting them to the sober conversation to come. "Now that we are so close to our dream, I am worried about how I will handle Inge and Jorg after you two are redeemed," she said, "What you think I should do? How will I take care of them and feed them?"

"I guess I thought you would be able to come with one of us, no matter where we go," Wilhelm said. He looked very serious. "I realize now that may not happen." Worry crossed his face; he would be upset if Katja thought he, the oldest brother, had let her down.

"Hans really wants to marry you, Katja," replied Peter. He took her hand and looked at her with a serious expression. "Consider that. He has spoken with us about it often."

"I have thought about it. He would be a better choice than trying to find my way alone," she said weighing the possibilities. "I have known him as a friend many years, and I have always liked him. He would be good with Inge and Jorg."

"He has asked us many times to speak for him. We just didn't know what you would want; you never said anything about the idea," Wilhelm explained.

He put his hand on his sister's arm for a moment, turning her toward him. "He feels concerned that he has little to offer until they are established somewhere." Reflecting a bit more on the situation, he added, "Of course, we have no dowry to offer him either."

With a devilish look in his brotherly eye, Peter added, "He is better than that Josef Wurfel who used to live on the farm next door. He had a brown eye and a blue eye! He asked us six times for your hand when you were only fourteen! He loved you, Katja!" He slapped his knee and doubled over laughing.

"He was short, dirty, square,little man, too. You would have had elves for kids!" laughed Wilhelm."Ha Ha Ha"

"Oh, you two! Stop! I need sensible advice from my brothers!" She gave them both a look as though she were correcting ill-behaved children.

"Well, our advice is agree to marry Hans, even if he has little to offer right now. He will do fine in Amerika. The two of them will have a store set up in no time, Jakob will soon find a wife, and you will all make a happy life,"

Wilhelm smiled. He thought to himself that Katja may actually do better than he and Peter.

Katja sat silently thinking this over. "I will accept his offer," Katja decided. Having made the choice, a good feeling swept over her. She and Hans had been friends for many years and knew each other well. She just never considered him, or anyone else, as a husband before this voyage. Life will be different here. "A great load is lifted from my shoulders and I feel very happy. You are good brothers," she said, giving them each a hug.

"We will go find him and tell him you have accepted him." Peter announced happily. He was pleased with the decision and knew it was good.

When Hans heard the news, he came immediately to Katja. "At last," he smiled and put his arm around her, "I been working on this since last winter! I am so happy! I like the idea of having Inge and Jorg, too! I am glad to start my new life in Amerika as a family man."

When Katja saw the expression on his face, she knew this was the right decision. She leaned against him feeling safe and comfortable. "I am happy, too," she smiled up at him.

Jakob was delighted with the news, "Hans has been talking about this so long, I was getting tired of listening to him!" He gave her a hug, "It will be good to have you with us, Katja."

Jakob continued, "We think we are going to go toward

western Chester County to the area called Lancaster Plain. Everyone we have talked to tells us they think we could do well there. There is a small population living there now and good opportunities for business."

"Let's go and tell Jorg and Inge about our plans," smiled Katja. "I know they will be delighted!" She took Hans by the hand and went looking for the young ones.

Philadelphia

Forty-Two

AT SUNRISE THE NEXT day, land could be seen on the distant horizon. Before the day was over, the *Good Queen* was approaching the Delaware Bay. Anchor was dropped at the mouth of the river awaiting the next dawn which would begin the last part of their ocean journey.

Seabirds wheeled overhead, delighting the passengers with their squawking cries.

Children were running over the deck, happily playing games and enjoying the summer evening.

Occasionally a fish jumped out of the water. Even the breezes seemed to welcome them from their long, difficult voyage.

❀   ❀   ❀

Captain Martin called everyone to the deck to check the list of the passengers as he planned his arrival in Philadelphia. He carefully marked beside each name their various situations -- fees paid, redemption necessary, ill, deceased, orphaned, newborn, etc.

He announced, "It will take several days to get to Philadelphia. It is about one hundred miles upstream. Those people who are to be redeemed may not disembark ship until payment is made. Each man on board will have to sign an Oath of Allegiance to the Crown of England, denouncing allegiance to your homeland. The ones who have paid the passage in full may leave after you have taken the oath and checked with Mr. Worthington, the same officer with whom you checked in and out while in England. If you are ill, you will have to be examined by a doctor before you are released."

❀　❀　❀

When the Captain left them, most passengers remained on deck, their eyes glued on their future homeland with shores of swamps, marshes, and occasional white sand stretches in the foreground with low natural growth in the distance and some trees farther inland. They were intrigued by the wilderness of the scene.

Hans turned to Jakob, "I think I counted more than fifteen passengers on his list 'tot am See'. (Dead at Sea) Most of them were mothers and children or older people over forty."

"Ja," said Katja, "It makes me feel very sad for the ones left behind. "

"It makes me feel fortunate that our little group from

Mosbach has been relatively lucky by comparison, even though we, too, have had some sad losses," noted Jakob.

The passengers standing nearby were full of excitement. Jakob, Hans, and Katja could hear them exchanging their plans and dreams with the other passengers as they stood in the group close-at-hand.

"We will meet my wife's family here and they will help get us settled! We will have our own land in a few years!" remarked the shoemaker to Jakob.

"I am going to get off this ship and just start walking west as far as I can go!" said another, a sturdy young man who looked like he could walk for quite a distance west.

"I am going to find some mules and stop at the first good farmland I find!" said Johannes Braun, holding the hand of his small son. "My boy will grow up to have land of his own!"

Herr Bachman said, "It is a bakery I am looking for. I want to join a baker in Philadelphia and work my way to a shop of my own." He looked so happy Hans had to smile at him and wish him success.

"I am worried about what to do," one wife said looking up at her husband, Karl. "We don't even know where the roads lead, nor, if there are places to stay with our families."

Another woman behind her agreed, "It is certainly easier if you are in a group like the Mennonites. Those of us who are just a family have a harder time." She was the woman from Heidelberg whose husband was a farmer.

A young mother who stood near Katja cried out with relief in her voice, "I, for one, am just glad to have survived this awful voyage." She hugged her youngest to her. "At least we all have made it here, safely!"

"Why do we have to sign a loyalty oath to the King of England? I am not English!" asked Heinrich Hirsch, an older man who seemed to think that Jakob would have an answer to his angry question.

Other passengers were strangely quiet, a bit fearful of the unknown, thinking to themselves, "What shall we do first? Shall we just start on a road to somewhere? Where?"

A mixture of happiness, relief, and apprehension settled on them all.

Forty-Three

The next morning the excited passengers stood in small groups at the ship's railing trying to get a better look at the shore along the Delaware River as they entered it from the bay.

Gerhardt Dietrich observed as they moved up river, "It reminds me a little of the Rhine -- wide, smooth flowing."

"I hate to say it but it makes me just a bit of homesick," remarked the weaver behind him. "A tiny heartache for a sight I will never see again."

"I have noticed a number of sandbars," said Jakob. "The Captain and crew have done a good job of steering clear of them."

"Yes, look over there. Do you see the small boat that seems to be grounded on a sandbar waiting for the tide to lift it!" Peter indicated a boat over near the shore. "I can see that a captain must stay to the deep water in the middle and keep a sharp eye out for shifting sands."

"That one on the starboard side looks like a cargo ship. It is smaller than we are," Hans observed, "but bigger than Captain Jager's river boat."

Jorg began shouting and pointing into the growth across the river. "Look over in the trees! It is an animal! It's a deer, I think!" Everyone's eyes followed his direction, but the animal turned, flashed its white tail, and disappeared.

The children were delighted to see the deer and spent the next hour lined along the railing looking for another.

"Here we will be able to hunt the deer without permission from the Prince!" Jorg overheard Herr Huber, who was standing behind him.

"Is that true?" Jorg asked Hans looking up at him with a surprised expression.

"It is true, Jorg, there is no Prince here."

Jorg was amazed. He was used to having his life controlled by some higher, more powerful person. Immediately, he loved Amerika. "No Prince! I never thought there *was* a place with no Prince!"

Then another thought struck Jorg. "We haven't seen any castles here either have we?" He had gotten used to seeing the numerous castles that sat on the high hilltops all along the Rhine River.

"No castles, Jorg. No Prince," repeated Hans, delighting in this little boy's amazement.

"How can that be?" Jorg reached inside his shirt and touched Grandfather's stone. "Did you hear that, Grandfather? No Castles! No Princes! You would be amazed, Grandfather!"

Forty-Four

THE ONE HUNDRED MILES to Philadelphia seemed to go quickly. About the fourth day, they sailed through a summer thunderstorm but most of them just stood on the deck and enjoyed the warm rain. It was refreshing to have the sea salt washed away. A few put out a bowl or two for a refreshing drink of water that didn't taste like a wooden keg.

When they were within hearing distance of Philadelphia, the sailors fired one of the cannons into the wilderness at the water's edge. The announcement would bring people to the wharf to see who was on board. It was a signal for friends and family who had come to meet a certain passenger. It was a signal for business men and farmers who were looking for workers.

The firing made the passengers realize they were very near to Philadelphia. They cried out, "Thank, God!" Praise His Name!" Laughing and rejoicing in loud celebration, they hugged each other, thankful that they had made it.

"Amazing!" was the word for the first site of Philadelphia. Wide-eyed, Jorg asked, "Where is the city wall? Is there no city wall?"

"No, son, William Penn did not need a city wall here," Gerhardt Dietrich replied. He was standing right behind Jorg admiring the port of Philadelphia, thinking to himself, "It is a good sign of hearty business."

"The streets are muddy from the rain," remarked his wife who was beside him. "That will seem like home!"

"Ah, the streets are muddy, but see how broad they are!" Gerhardt added. "I can see that the Penn family has laid this city out according to a plan! It didn't just grow along a cross on the road, like our towns and villages did!"

Jorg noticed something else. He turned to Dietrich and said, "Look! It is laid out in squares like Mannheim, the city we saw along the Rhine!"

Gerhardt agreed, "It certainly is, Jorg. This is a planned city."

"Everything looks new!" Frau Braun remarked to the group. "Are there no old buildings here?"

"It is much bigger than I thought," said a carpenter from Rothenberg gazing out at the buildings, and businesses. "I guess I supposed it would be a smaller town. Do you know how big it is, Dietrich?"

Gerhardt Dietrich, probably one of the most educated on

board, said, "I have read there were about 20,000 people here in Philadelphia by the count they made in 1717."

"Twenty thousand!" some of the voices echoed unbelievingly.

"I smell horses and I hear carts," remarked another man. "That is a good sign of a busy port. And, it smells like LAND, my boy!" He happily gave Jorg a hug just to share his happiness.

Jorg reached into his purse and took Grandfather's smooth stone into his hand. He whispered, "We are here, Grandfather. Can you see Philadelphia? We made it! Oh! how I wish you were here, too!"

❀   ❀   ❀

The crew easily got the ship positioned by the Market Street Wharf, one of the busiest. Shipping companies and businesses both large and small were all around the area. Carts, horses, people and animals were everywhere! People were selling fish, baked goods, wheat, flour, leather goods, dishes -- everything one could want.

Then, just as Amos and Mathias predicted, several small individual boats appeared in the water just below them. Some of the men in the boats were dressed in plain dark outfits like the Weber family, others in common clothes. They called up to the ship with the names of the people they were trying to find. "Amos! Mathias! Christian! Are you there?"

Amos grinned, "They promised they would come!" He shouted and waved to the ones he knew.

All had gifts which they passed up to the passengers -- fresh bread, apples, jugs of fresh water, boiled eggs, nuts, small pieces of cheese. Eager hands caught the offerings and passed them around.

The mothers on board tried to gather the family together so that none would be lost in the confusion and excitement. People were folding blankets, repacking trunks, getting ready to step onto the land as they had yearned to do for months.

About ten passengers were judged to be too sick to disembark. They had to go below and wait to be examined for contagious disease. Other family members waited with them, their demeanor clearly one of fright and trepidation. "What if they decide we cannot stay?" one mother asked as she held her sick child.

"Someone told me there is a shipping building where we are kept until we are well. Or, if we are sent back."

"None of us are so sick that a decent meal with some fresh meat or fruit wouldn't help us," one man commented angrily.

"No one has the pox," another father said loudly.

One of the ship's officers overheard the discussion and told them gruffly, "Just sit quiet now and don't cause a problem. You will be the last to be attended to."

Forty-Five

THE CAPTAIN'S FIRST MATE announced, "We have sent the Custom's House the list of names of the men on the *Good Queen*. We will take you to sign the Oath of Allegiance now."

"Every male sixteen and over line up here," another officer said.

The men lined up. All women, children, and belongings had to remain on board. Mr. Worthington lead the way to the Court House with the Captain, and his staff positioning themselves around the passengers, making sure none left the group or got lost in the crowded market streets.

At the Court House the Oath of Allegiance was read to them in English by an official of the Province, dressed in a powdered wig and a fancy fawn-colored coat, a ruffled shirt, and green pants that ended at his knee. He had high stockings that came up to meet the pants. Wilhelm and Peter exchanged glances when they saw his outfit.

The Oath was a two page document denouncing James of Scotland and swearing allegiance to George, the son of Queen Anne, and his successors. All who could write their names did so.

Mr. Worthington, the Captain, or a friend wrote for those who could not write or who could write only their initials. Each passenger made his mark beside it.

"I will write your name, Wilhelm and Peter, and you must put your mark," said Hans to the brothers.

"Thank you, Hans," they said, glad that a friend could do this for them.

"Line up over here after you sign and we will return to the ship," announced the Captain.

They marched back exactly as they had come, a dirty, ragged, sometimes barefoot, worn-out looking group but now with big smiles spread across their faces.

With that done, those who had paid their fare in full began to gather their belongings; families prepared to disembark.

❀　❀　❀

The return to ship was a time of parting for the Meier family, the Holtzmanns, and the Kramers. None were quite sure what to say as they stood together holding on to each other. For months they had waited for this moment, now it seemed too fast!

"We have been side by side since February, Barbara," Katja cried, hugging her friend. "Oh, how I will miss you! I am happy for you and for young Rudi and Magdalena, too."

"We have been through so much together," said Ulrich. "We must not part forever. We have too many memories. " He put an arm around Wilhelm and added, "It seems so long ago that we sat in your shed and told you to get some information when you took Overlord Frederich's grain to the market!"

Barbara and Ulrich, each with a child beside them, looked at their long time friends. "We knew we would part someday, but now it seems so difficult," said Barbara. Tears were in her eyes. "It has been a lifetime!"

"We are heading into the city of Philadelphia to find a carpenter shop that needs some help. That is where you will find us," said Ulrich.

"Look for a wonderful carpenter and his talented son," smiled Rudi. He helped Ulrich lift the trunk, getting ready to carry it off the ship.

The others watched them as they were checked out with Mr. Worthington. Their eyes followed as the four of them began their journey toward the city center. They were kept in sight until they disappeared down the street of Philadelphia called Chestnut.

"We know where Hans, Katja, and Jacob are headed -- to

the Lancaster Plain. When we are free, we will come there, too," Wilhelm vowed.

"Yes," Peter agreed. "Wilhelm and I do not know what is in store for us, but we have sworn to each other to find our way back together again."

Forty-Six

KATJA STOOD BETWEEN HER brothers and Hans. She never dreamed this would be so hard. There was never a time in their lives when they were separated. Tears were flowing down her cheeks. Jorg and Inge clung to Wilhelm and Peter. "When we planned this we always thought how wonderful it would be in a new land. We didn't think about how it would be when we would have to part from each other!"

Tears stung Jorg's eyes as he said, "Please look for us in five years. I will be older than Daniel was when we last saw him."

Inge kissed Wilhelm and Peter and laughed, "Maybe I will be married to a handsome man in five years!"

"At age nine! You had better not, Little One. Peter and I will come and chase him off!" laughed Wilhelm hugging her to him. He would miss this bright little piece of sunshine in his life.

"You remember, Jorg, you are the one who must write to Daniel so he can find you if he comes to Amerika as a sea captain!" Peter added. He was very proud of the way his little brother worked so hard with Hans during the voyage to learn to read and write just for that very reason.

Jakob, who had gone off to buy a small wagon and horse for traveling, and carrying trunks, returned with a slow, grey-muzzled mule and a small four-wheeled horse cart. "All I could find was this small cart and this old jenny, but I am sure it will get us there." He scratched her old grey head and laughed. "Her name is Honig."

They loaded the two trunks into the cart and lifted the two children into the back.

Katja had separated the things in the Meier trunk so that the brothers each had a rucksack with their own things. Without telling them, she put all the money they still had in with their belongings. It was only a few shillings, but it was better than none.

Jakob clucked Honig into a walk and they began their journey toward the Lancaster Plain.

Wilhelm and Peter stood side by side with each other on deck. They had to remain on board until someone came and paid their fees.

A doctor appeared on the wharf, hitching his small cart to a post near the ship. He came onto the deck. "I am here to do some examinations," he said. "If you are sick stay over on that side. I am going to look at the redemptioners first so they can be sold."

Forty-Seven

WILHELM, PETER, AND ABOUT twelve others stayed together waiting for the examination. The doctor was very quick, taking each man in turn, simply checking for disease or obvious defects which would prevent him from working for his buyer.

When he was finished he said, "Mr. Worthington, these men are all ready to be sold for their fees." He turned to the group and instructed them, "Move over by Mr. Worthington; he will take care of you now. "

The doctor turned his attention to the sick. With this group he was also looking for potentially fatal diseases which could become a serious threat, such as small pox, typhoid, or measles.

❁   ❁   ❁

There were plenty of people milling around the dock, planning to hire the redemptioners for a given number of years. When the doctor released them, interested buyers came onboard to look over the possibilities.

One very well-dressed man came with his wife, who was looking for a young woman to be a nanny to their children. They purchased a woman whose husband had died on board therefore forcing her to pay double the years. They also took her small daughter; however, they refused to take her older son who was about fourteen. The boy's mother had no choice. She wiped away her tears, hugged him, and said, "I will search for you, Samuel. Work hard and do your best. You will get along well that way."

Wilhelm stood close to Peter and watched the little family being broken up. "I realize now, how lucky for Katja that she went with Hans. That could have our family."

The buyer took the woman and her small child with them as they headed to the market stands, leaving the older boy standing dejectedly near the brothers, his hands clutched into fists to help him control his tears.

As they waited, Wilhelm began to feel anxious. "I worry that we do not speak the language, or understand the customs," frowned Wilhelm. "Sometimes I do not always understand what is being asked of me -- like when we signed the Oath of Allegiance."

"Look around, brother," Peter put his hand on Wilhelm's arm. "Do you see any castles? Overlords? Soldiers? Prince Electors? We survived all of them! We must have faith and courage! Most of these people are just like us -- looking for a chance to make a good life for themselves! We can do this!"

Forty-Eight

"You, there, what is your name?" a well-dressed man in knee-high leather boots stopped and stood in front of Wilhelm. He spoke in German to him. He liked these young Germans; they made good workers.

Immediately Wilhelm felt better and answered, "Wilhelm Meier, Sir."

"Were you a farmer, son?" asked Thomas Rutter.

"Ja."

"I live a long way from here -- out toward the frontier. I am working with some partners to establish Colebrookdale Furnace near Iron Stone Creek, in the Schuylkill Valley. Does that mean anything to you?"

"No, but I am a good worker. I can learn to do any kind of work."

"Can you cut down trees and make charcoal?"

"I can cut down trees. I will learn to make charcoal."

"Good! That is what I want to hear. This will be a five year agreement, do you understand?"

"Yes, Sir."

He turned to Mr. Worthington and said, "I will pay for this man, Wilhelm Meier." He paid six pounds for Wilhelm.

Mr. Worthington took the fee, recorded it, and said, "Thank you Mr. Rutter. Good luck now. Have a good trip back."

Mr. Rutter lingered, continuing to survey the group. "I need at least one more man," he said. "Running an iron furnace is hard work." He looked around at the others. "I need someone young and strong."

"My brother is here, Sir," said Wilhelm quietly, pointing to Peter, who was being interviewed by a stout, bearded Swede named Mouns Jones who had settled on the shores the Schuylkill beyond the Manatawny Creek.

"Well, Jones, you going to take that man or not? I need him for my iron furnace," Mr. Rutter called to him.

"I am, Rutter, find yourself another one," answered Mr. Jones, amused at the way Rutter always acted like he was the boss. He turned to Peter and said, "If that is your brother, you won't be far apart. Rutter is establishing an iron furnace not too many miles downriver from me."

"That would be fine, Sir," smiled Peter delighted to hear the news. "I am a good worker. You say you want land cleared, trees cut, stumps pulled, plowing done? I can do that Sir."

"I will pay for this man, Peter Meier," said Jones turning to Mr. Worthington who told him the price would be six pounds.

As Mr. Rutter went off to look at some of the other young men, Peter and Wilhelm hugged each other overjoyed by their good fortune.

"We have just had a great piece of luck, brother! Within miles of each other is better than I ever dreamed!" Peter was happy, a great burden lifted from his heart.

"I will find you before summer is over, Wilhelm," Peter promised.

Mr. Rutter returned with Samuel, the boy of fourteen years, who had gotten split from his family during the hiring. The family had come from the town of Worms.

Mr. Rutter said to Samuel, "Since you are only fourteen, you will have to stay with me until you are twenty. Do you understand that?"

Samuel nodded, then asked, "Mr. Rutter, could you find out the name of the man who paid for my mother and little sister?"

"I can do that," he smiled and walked over to the man and wife who hired Samuel's mother, and requested that information.

Upon his return he handed a paper with the information to Samuel. "Do you have a purse to put this in son? The next time I come to Philadelphia I will bring you with me so you can visit. It is not far from here."

Samuel smiled. For the first time, he thought this may work out after all.

They stopped at a small stand near the wharf to buy something to eat, for it was a long ride home. The three newly hired fellows relished the fresh bread, meat, and vegetables. They gulped down the milk. Each ate an apple or two.

"Well, I can see Master Martin is up to his old tricks! Half starving you to save money!" laughed Rutter.

"When you taste my Ingeborg's stew, you'll forget that terrible food you had to eat on board!" grinned Jones.

Forty-Nine

THEY ALL MOUNTED THE horses the buyers had brought along and began the ride west through the city. When the met the broad Schuylkill River, they took the narrow road that led along the water, staying together as a group. The road was not much more than a generous path winding through the shade trees beside the wide river.

Mouns Jones told them about himself as they rode. "I was born here. My father got land from William Penn. My wife, Ingeborg, and I have two children, a little older than you Peter. We are trying to develop this land for farming."

Thomas Rutter also told them about his iron works near the Manatawny Creek called Colebrookdale Furnace. "We have just finished the furnace this year. We will be producing iron ore into pig metal. Do you know what that is?"

Wilhelm and Samuel couldn't help laughing at the name,

but soon found that it was the material used by all the other iron workers, such as blacksmiths.

"You and Samuel will work hard," Rutter continued, "but you will learn a lot about making iron. We cast much of our iron into implements."

Mr. Jones and Mr. Rutter were happy with their new workers. They had found strong young men willing to work for them the next five years, building the properties they were developing.

However, none could have been happier than the two brothers who rode side by side along the quiet forest lane.

Epilogue 1771

As the house filled with the good aromas of "suppertime" the children gathered around Jorg's chair by the fireplace.

"Tell us again, Grandpa, how that white stone got from a small stream in Germany to our mantle here in Amerika." The little ones sat on Jorg's lap and around his rocking chair waiting in anticipation to hear yet again the story they had heard a dozen times before.

Again, Jorg told them of his boyhood in Germany, his family, of their exciting, and often frightening, journey to Amerika. He told of how hard it was to part when they reached Philadelphia.

"Are they all still in Lancaster?" asked little Jorg, his namesake.

Grandpa Jorg smiled as he remembered once more how the family set up the store among the Mennonites as they began their business in Lancaster.

"Jakob married, but he and his wife died of illness leaving

no heirs. Sister Katja and Hans had three sons and three daughters, who still live in Lancaster."

"Do they still have the General Store?" asked young Peter.

"In the last letter I received from Hans he wrote, *We are both well, but getting too old to run the store, so our youngest son is going to take over the business.* "

"What happened to your little sister, Inge?" asked Peter's little sister, Eliza.

"Inge married and had many sons," he answered.

"Where are they now?" she pressed him for more.

Inge and her husband, Nicholaus, have moved to land west of the Susquehanna River, near a mountain called South Mountain. It is part of the Pennsylvania county called Cumberland. "

"Tell us again about your brother, Daniel. Did he become a sea captain?" asked the older boy at Jorg's knee who was the image of his namesake, Wilhelm.

"Ah… Daniel." Jorg stroked his beard, smiled, and leaned back in his rocking chair, remembering. "I wrote to Daniel several times a year, but many years passed before we saw him again. When he became a sea captain, he found Ulrich and Barbara with their family in Philadelphia. That is how he found us in Lancaster."

"Did he stay with you in Lancaster?" asked the big sister, Catherina.

"Daniel loved the sea. He established his own shipping company in Philadelphia when he got older. He is gone now, but his sons still have the business."

"Did you ever see your big brothers, Wilhelm and Peter, again?" asked little Eliza.

"Wilhelm and Peter came to Lancaster after their five years of redemption were finished. Then they took a land warranty in the Tulpehocken area. That is called Berks County now. There they married and had families."

"Tell us about the Indian attack, too!" Little Peter urged Grandpa Jorg. He always asked to hear this part because his namesake uncle was one of the heroes.

"Well, Peter and Wilhelm's families were attacked by Indians who raided the area in 1750. Peter saved all the children by sneaking them out through a secret tunnel from the root cellar. He hid them in the forest, but Wilhelm and his wife were killed while trying to save the property and give the others a chance to escape."

Jorg always felt sad when he remembered the death of Wilhelm, the one who always took care of everyone. That was the way he lived, and that was the way he died.

Grandpa Jorg continued, "Peter was too sad to live there any longer, so he and his wife took all the children -- his and Wilhelm's --- and moved west of the Susquehanna River to a place called Little Buffalo Creek. That is not too far from Inge."

"Is Uncle Peter still alive?" asked young Peter.

"Uncle Peter is a very old man, now. He is nearly seventy. He lives with his daughter and her family."

"We love when you share these things with us, Grandpa Jorg. We are going to grow up and share all these stories with our children, too, so they will know how we became part of this country. Our family memories will never die!"

When the grandchildren were called to the supper table, Jorg took the white stone into his old hand, and said very quietly to himself, "As long as they remember, you will never be forgotten. Did you hear that, Grandfather? Wilhelm? Jakob? Daniel?"

And, in his heart, he knew they did.

Historical Background

RESEARCHING MY FAMILY ROOTS which are in Germany, Switzerland, England, Wales, and Alsace, took me into the seventeenth and eighteenth centuries. I was intrigued as I learned of the sacrifices and the dangers immigrants faced in coming to America. In my own opinion, the dangers were far more than the ones faced by astronauts going into space, for the support system was absent, the dangers were unpredictable, and there was little chance of rescue or help. Although this story is fictional, the situations the characters face are based on the true adventures of my ancestors and hundreds of other families who were courageous enough to face a future filled with multitudinous unknowns.

Why did Europeans come to America in boatloads? Most would reply - religious freedom. Certainly, that was one reason. Of course, those immigrants who were persecuted such as the Huguenots, the Mennonites, and the Quakers were looking for the religious freedom promised by William Penn. Lutheranism and Catholicism battled back and forth across Europe for hundreds of years in an effort to control of the hearts and minds of the people. Most rulers required allegiance to a certain religion, while a few were tolerant if it was financially worth their while.

The Thirty Years War, in the first half of the 1600's, left a devastated Europe in its wake. Invading armies burned homes and destroyed crops and farm animals. Sometimes entire villages were destroyed, leaving behind homeless families, orphans, disease, and starvation. Most of the second half of the 1600's were spent trying to recover from this devastation.

Beginning in 1688, before full recovery could be achieved, King Louis XIV of France once again sent troops into the Palatinate area along the Rhine to win it for France. Once again the people of the area suffered yet another army surging through their land. In 1701-1714, the Spanish armies followed the French with the War of Spanish Succession sweeping across the same area.

In the early 1700's, Germany was a collection of nearly 300 small principalities, duchies, and city states which were each ruled by a rich family who owned the farm land and villages. The people were taxed to the limit of their endurance.

Ruling with an iron hand, Princes and Kings controlled most aspects of the people's lives including religion, income, travel, social rules such as who could marry, and the kind of work in which a person could be engaged. The system kept the farmers and craftsmen subject to the will of the rich, insuring that the peasants would remain poor, uneducated, and without hope of owning land or achieving self-determination.

These German Princes fought with each other constantly, vying for dominance over the land. Each Prince wanted authority over the Neckar, the Mainz, and the Mosel Rivers which flowed into the Rhine. In the east, they sought control of the Danube River. Rulers had their soldiers stationed along the river; when a ship passed, they extended chains across the river and collected fees before allowing a boat to continue its journey.

The weather itself became the enemy when the winters of 1708 and 1709 and the immediate years following, brought the area a devastatingly cold weather period. Extreme cold arrived in September and by November rivers were frozen, fruit trees were killed, farm animals froze where they stood. Starvation and hardship spread across the land, the effects of which lasted years because crops were killed before they could be harvested, and before seed could be saved for planting the next year.

A mass exodus took place, especially in Switzerland and western Germany near the Rhine River, from the early 1700's through the 1760's.

America, especially Pennsylvania, offered a chance to begin again, to own your own land, obtain an education, create wealth, and enjoy self determination. William Penn invited German farmers to populate his colony; he promised religions of all kinds would be tolerated. His sons continued their father's policies.

The world has never had a short supply of crooks, and so, came the Newlanders, like a hoard of locusts, feeding on the troubles of the poor German peasant farmers. Newlanders were hired by the ship captains to get people to sign on to come to America. They dressed well and enticed the poor, starved, frozen farmers of the Palatinate with stories of fortune, promising them a land of Eden if they signed up to go to America. What the Newlanders didn't tell them was that they were paid by the captain per capita for every adult passenger signed and boarded. The captain then redeemed these passengers to farmers or tradesmen in America to recover their fees at a profit.

These German and Swiss peasants, called Redemptioners, were required to sign papers they could not read and did not understand. Even the few who could read discovered the papers were often in English, not German. Ship captains soon learned that the terrible conditions aboard ship would mean death to a percentage of their living cargo, so they filled the passenger area with extra people to adjust for the predicted loss. Captains also enforced the rule: if a Redemptioner died after the half-way point of the voyage, his kin had to work out that person's fees in addition to their own. The Captain decided where the half-way point was.

The Rhine River rises in the Swiss Alps and flows northward, making the border of Alsace, France, and Baden-Wurttemberg. It continues its northward journey, bordering the area called the Palatinate, until finally, near Mainz, it makes a great elbow turn and heads directly toward the North Sea, where it separates into numerous channels and flows into the Netherlands. As it enters the sea at Rotterdam, it forms a delta made up of many islands and channels.

In Rotterdam, ship captains loaded and unloaded trade goods from all over the known world, then traveled on to England, stopping at one of the port cities such as Liverpool, Portsmouth, or Cowes. There they picked up more trade goods, mail, and supplies for the colonies before heading westward. The captain obtained permission from England to land in America.

Ships crossed the Atlantic loaded with trade goods in the cargo space. Passengers were crowded into an extra space built between the original decks especially for them. The voyage to America for these peasants was a 'no frills' ride with very few amenities.

If the weather cooperated and the captain was honest, the trip could take six to eight weeks. If they met storms, high winds, bad conditions, or dishonest captains the voyage could last two to three months. There are documented cases on record in which the trip took as much as twelve weeks.

To Read More On This Subject

Early Eighteenth Century Palatine Emigration. by Walter A. Knittle 1965

Eighteenth Century Emigrants. Register of Emigrants From Southern Germany. Edited by Prof Werner Hacker. 1994

Eighteenth Century Emigrants from Northern Alsace to America by Annette K Burgert. 1992

German Immigration Into Pennsylvania by Frank Ried Diffenderffer. 1979

Immigrants in American History: Arrival, Adaptation, and Integration By Elliott Robert Barkan

Lists of Swiss Emigrants in the Eighteenth Century to the American Colonies. Edited by Faust and Brumbaugh. 1968 (Two Volumes in One)

Palatine Origins of Some Pennsylvania Pioneers by Annette K Burgert. 2000

Palatine Origins of Some Pennsylvania Pioneers. by Annette Kunselman Burgert. 2000

Pennsylvania German Immigrant 1709-1786 Edited by Don Yoder. 1984

Thirty Thousand Names of Immigrants in Pennsylvania by Daniel Rupp. 1965

Books On Google Play

(These books can be read on Google Play for free because they are out of copyright.)

A Collection of Upwards Thirty Thousand Names of German,, Swiss, Dutch, French and Other Immigrants in Pennsylvania From 1727 to 1776. by Daniel Rupp. 1896 (Books on Google Play)

History of Cumberland and Adams Counties Pennsylvania. 1886. (Books on Google Play)

History of the Mennonites by Daniel Kolb Cassel. 1888 (Books on Google Play)

History of Lehigh County. 1914. (Books on Google Play)

Life and Letters of John Philip Boehm. Published by the Reformed Church of USA. 1916 (Books on Google Play)

Penn Germania. 1914 (Books on Google Play)

Pennsylvania Genealogies by William Henry Egle. 1886 (Books on Google Play)

Redemptioners and Indentured Servants in Colony and Commonwealth. by Karl Frederick Geiser. 1901 (Books on Google Play)

Internet Sources

Eighteenth Century History of Germany. Wikipedia.

Eighteenth Century German Emigration Research. by Gary Horiacher. 2000

Gottlieb Mittelberger's Journey to Pennsylvania, 1754

Western Civilization. 3rd Edition. "Eighteenth Century Social Order: Peasants and Aristos" Jackson Spielvogel.

Brobst Chronicles, hosted by roots web

note:

The above suggestions are only a few of such resources. Your local historic society or genealogy society will have many more.

About the Author

Sʜɪʀʟᴇʏ A Kɪᴛɴᴇʀ Mᴀɪɴᴇʟʟᴏ is a retired educator who was a classroom teacher, reading specialist, school administrator, and private tutor.

Since retiring she has become involved in writing, traveling, photography, and genealogy.

Like Grandpa Jorg at the end of this story, her childhood was filled with stories of people who came before; stories which inspired her to learn to know her ancestors as real people living through real life struggles.

Her travels have taken her to Germany several times, visiting many of the small towns along the Rhine and in the Palatinate area, Switzerland, and Alsace.

Books By This Author

<u>**There Are Roads......**</u>

An inspirational photo story. Great as a gift book

<u>**Snooty the Reading Dog**</u>

<u>**Snooty the Reading Dog Learns About the Library**</u>

Both of these books are written for children ages six to nine. They entertain while teaching a concept.

<u>**We'll Love You Forever**</u>

An easy to read dog story written for children grades three to five.

<u>**Touching Lives.**</u>

A book written about her educational career.

To learn more about these books, visit her website :

www.storiesbysam.net

She welcomes email at the address below; write **BOOKS** in the subject line

sakitner.mainello@yahoo.com

You can purchase these books on amazon.com. Search by author name: Kitner-Mainello

Book Club Guidelines

1. Each of these families have a slightly different background. How did this background influence their individual responses to the difficulties faced? Consider: response to the Captain's demands, the soldier's demands, the way they responded to the reactions of those in power, the response to people in need.

2. Discuss the characters themselves and the decisions they made. For example: Daniel, Captain Jager, Katja, Ulrich and Barbara.

3. Had you been the one to make this trip, is there a point at which you would have turned back? When? What would have made you decide this?

   If you had continued on what would have been the joys and trials of the trip for you? What would have been the consequences of this decision?

4. Which events impressed you greatly? This is a big question. Be sure to explain your reasoning.

5. What do you think are some of the most outstanding traits of these people in general?

6. At any point in this story, did you go to the computer to see if this was true? What motivated that action?

7. Would you recommend this book to another reader? Why? Why not?

8. Where in this story were you impressed with:

   morality or the lack thereof
   courage
   depth of character
   resilience

9. If you liked this book and would like to make a written statement about it on Amazon, go the book write up itself and indicate your wish.

10. Questions or thoughts can be emailed to the author at *sakitner.mainello@yahoo.com* Put **BOOK** in the subject line.